THE PRISONER OF ZENDA

THE PRISONER OF ZENDA

Anthony Hope

Bloomsbury Books
London

This edition published 1994 by Bloomsbury Books, an
imprint of The Godfrey Cave Group, 42 Bloomsbury Street,
London, WC1B 3QJ.

ISBN 1 85471 217 9

Printed and bound by Firmin-Didot (France),
Group Herissey. No d'impression : 27111.

Contents

1 The Rassendylls—with a Word on the Elphbergs   7

2 Concerning the Colour of Men's Hair   13

3 A Merry Evening with a Distant Relative   20

4 The King keeps his Appointment   28

5 The Adventures of an Understudy   35

6 The Secret of a Cellar   42

7 His Majesty sleeps in Strelsau   49

8 A Fair Cousin and a Dark Brother   56

9 A New Use for a Tea Table   64

10 A Great Chance for a Villain   72

11 Hunting a Very Big Boar   79

12 I receive a Visitor and bait a Hook   87

13 An Improvement on Jacob's Ladder   94

14 A Night outside the Castle   101

15 I talk with a Tempter   108

16 A Desperate Plan   115

17 Young Rupert's Midnight Diversions   122

18 The Forcing of the Trap   128

19 Face to Face in the Forest   134

20 The Prisoner and the King   140

21 If Love were All!   147

22 Present, Past—and Future?   154

1

The Rassendylls—with a Word on the Elphbergs

"I wonder when in the world you're going to do anything, Rudolf?" said my brother's wife.

"My dear Rose," I answered, laying down my egg spoon, "why in the world should I do anything? My position is a comfortable one. I have an income nearly sufficient for my wants (no one's income is ever quite sufficient, you know). I enjoy an enviable social position. I am brother to Lord Burlesdon, and brother-in-law to that most charming lady his countess. Behold, it is enough!"

"You are nine-and-twenty," she observed, "and you've done nothing but—"

"Knock about? It is true. Our family doesn't need to do things."

This remark of mine rather annoyed Rose, for everybody knows (and therefore there can be no harm in referring to the fact) that, pretty and accomplished as she herself is, her family is hardly of the same standing as the Rassendylls. Besides her attractions, she possessed a large fortune, and my brother Robert was wise enough not to mind about her ancestry. Ancestry is, in fact, a matter concerning which the next observation of Rose's has some truth.

"Good families are generally worse than any others," she said.

Upon this I stroked my hair. I knew quite well what she meant.

"I'm so glad Robert's is black!" she cried.

At this moment Robert (who rises at seven and works before breakfast) came in. He glanced at his wife. Her cheek was slightly flushed. He patted it caressingly.

"What's the matter, my dear?" he asked.

"She objects to my doing nothing and having red hair," said I in an injured tone.

"Oh! Of course he can't help his hair," admitted Rose.

"It generally crops out once in a generation," said my brother. "So does the nose. Rudolf has got them both."

"I wish they didn't crop out," said Rose, still flushed.

"I rather like them myself," said I, and, rising, I bowed to the portrait of Countess Amelia.

My brother's wife uttered an exclamation of impatience.

"I wish you'd take that picture away, Robert," said she.

"My dear!" he cried.

"Good Heavens!" I added.

"Then it might be forgotten," she continued.

"Hardly—with Rudolf about," said Robert, shaking his head.

"Why should it be forgotten?" I asked.

"Rudolf!" exclaimed my brother's wife, blushing very prettily.

I laughed, and went on with my egg. At least I had shelved the question of what (if anything) I ought to do. And by way of closing the discussion—and also, I must admit, of exasperating my strict little sister-in-law a trifle more—I observed, "I rather like being an Elphberg myself."

When I read a story I skip the explanations, yet the moment I begin to write one I find that I must have an explanation. For it is manifest that I must explain why my sister-in-law was vexed with my nose and hair, and why I venture to call myself an Elphberg. For, eminent as, I must protest, the Rassendylls have been for many generations, yet participation in their blood of course does not, at first sight, justify the boast of a connection with the grander stock of the Elphbergs or a claim to be one of that royal house. For what relationship is there between Ruritania and Burlesdon, between the palace at Strelsau or the castle of Zenda and No. 305 Park Lane, W.

Well, then—and I must premise that I am going, perforce, to rake up the very scandal which my dear Lady Burlesdon wishes forgotten—in the year 1733, George II, sitting then on the throne, peace reigning for the moment, and the king and the Prince of

Wales being not yet at loggerheads, there came on a visit to the English court a certain prince who was afterwards known to history as Rudolf the Third of Ruritania. The prince was a tall, handsome young fellow, marked (maybe marred, it is not for me to say) by a somewhat unusually long, sharp, and straight nose, and a mass of dark-red hair—in fact, the nose and the hair which have stamped the Elphbergs time out of mind. He stayed some months in England, where he was most courteously received, yet in the end he left rather under a cloud. For he fought a duel (it was considered highly well bred of him to waive all question of his rank) with a nobleman, well known in the society of the day not only for his own merits but as the husband of a very beautiful wife. In that duel Prince Rudolf received a severe wound, and recovering therefrom, was adroitly smuggled off by the Ruritanian ambassador, who had found him a pretty handful. The nobleman was not wounded in the duel, but the morning being raw and damp on the occasion of the meeting, he contracted a severe chill, and failing to throw it off, he died some six months after the departure of Prince Rudolf, without having found leisure to adjust his relations with his wife—who after another two months bore an heir to the title and estates of the family of Burlesdon. This lady was the Countess Amelia, whose picture my sister-in-law wished to remove from the drawing room in Park Lane, and her husband was James, fifth Earl of Burlesdon and twenty-second Baron Rassendyll, both in the peerages of England, and a Knight of the Garter. As for Rudolf, he went back to Ruritania, married a wife and ascended the throne, whereon his progeny in the direct line have sat from then till this very hour—with one short interval. And, finally, if you walk through the picture galleries at Burlesdon, among the fifty portraits or so of the last century and a half you will find five or six, including that of the sixth earl, distinguished by long, sharp, straight noses and a quantity of dark-red hair. These five or six have also blue eyes, whereas among the Rassendylls dark eyes are the commoner.

That is the explanation, and I am glad to have finished it. The blemishes on honourable lineage are a delicate subject, and certainly this heredity we hear so much about is the finest scandalmonger in the world. It laughs at discretion and writes strange entries between the lines of the "Peerages".

It will be observed that my sister-in-law, with a want of logic that must have been peculiar to herself (since we are no longer allowed to lay it to the charge of her sex), treated my complexion almost as an offence for which I was responsible, hastening to assume from that external sign inward qualities of which I protest my entire innocence; and this unjust inference she sought to buttress by pointing to the uselessness of the life I had led. Well, be that as it may, I had picked up a good deal of pleasure and a good deal of knowledge. I had been to a German school and a German university, and spoke German as readily and perfectly as English. I was thoroughly at home in French. I had a smattering of Italian, and enough Spanish to swear by. I was, I believe, a strong, though hardly a fine, swordsman and good shot. I could ride anything that had a back to sit on, and my head was as cool a one as you could find, for all its flaming cover. If you say that I ought to have spent my time in useful labour I am out of court and have nothing to say, save that my parents had no business to leave me two thousand pounds a year and a roving disposition.

"The difference between you and Robert," said my sister-in-law, who often (bless her!) speaks on a platform, and oftener still as if she were on one, "is that he recognizes the duties of his position, and you only see the opportunities of yours."

"To a man of spirit, my dear Rose," I answered, "opportunities are duties."

"Nonsense!" said she, tossing her head, and after a moment she went on: "Now here's Sir Jacob Borrodaile offering you exactly what you might be equal to."

"A thousand thanks!" I murmured.

"He's to have an embassy in six months, and Robert says he is sure that he'll take you as an attaché. Do take it, Rudolf—to please me."

Now when my sister-in-law puts the matter in that way, wrinkling her pretty brows, twisting her little hands, and growing wistful in the eyes, all on account of an idle scamp like myself, for whom she has no natural responsibility, I am visited with compunction. Moreover, I thought it possible that I could pass the time in the position suggested with some tolerable amusement. Therefore I said, "My dear sister, if in six months' time no unforeseen obstacle has arisen, and Sir Jacob invites me, hang me if I don't go with Sir Jacob!"

"O Rudolf, how good of you! I am glad!"

"Where's he going to?"

"He doesn't know yet, but it's sure to be a good embassy."

"Madame," said I, "for your sake I'll go if it's no more than a beggarly legation. When I do a thing I don't do it by halves."

My promise, then, was given, but six months are six months and seem an eternity, and inasmuch as they stretched between me and my prospective industry (I suppose attachés are industrious, but I know not, for I never became attaché to Sir Jacob or to anybody else) I cast about for some desirable mode of spending them. And it occurred to me suddenly that I would visit Ruritania. It may seem strange that I had never visited that country yet, but my father (in spite of a sneaking fondness for the Elphbergs, which led him to give me, his second son, the famous Elphberg name of Rudolf) had always been averse to my going, and since his death my brother, prompted by Rose, had accepted the family tradition which taught that a wide berth was to be given to that country. But the moment Ruritania had come into my head I was eaten up with curiosity to see it. After all, red hair and long noses are not confined to the House of Elphberg, and the old story seemed a preposterously insufficient reason for debarring myself from acquaintance with a highly interesting and important kingdom, one which had played no small part in European history and might do the like again under the sway of a young and vigorous ruler, such as the new king was rumoured to be. My determination was clinched by reading in *The Times* that Rudolf the Fifth was to be crowned at Strelsau in the course of the next three weeks, and that great magnificence was to mark the occasion. At once I made up my mind to be present and began my preparations. But inasmuch as it has never been my practice to furnish my relatives with an itinerary of my journeys, and in this case I anticipated opposition to my wishes, I gave out that I was going

for a ramble in the Tyrol—an old haunt of mine—and propitiated
Rose's wrath by declaring that I intended to study the political
and social problems of the interesting community which dwells
in that neighbourhood.

"Perhaps," I hinted darkly, "there may be an outcome of the expedition."

"What do you mean?" she asked.

"Well," said I carelessly, "there seems a gap that might be filled
by an exhaustive work on—"

"Oh! Will you write a book?" she cried, clapping her hands.
"That would be splendid, wouldn't it, Robert?"

"It's the best of introductions to political life nowadays," observed my brother, who has, by the way, introduced himself in
this manner several times over. *Burlesdon on "Ancient Theories
and Modern Facts"* and *"The Ultimate Outcome," by a Political
Student* are both works of recognized eminence.

"I believe you are right, Bob, my boy," said I.

"Now promise you'll do it," said Rose earnestly.

"No, I won't promise, but if I find enough material I will."

"That's fair enough," said Robert.

"Oh! Material doesn't matter," she said, pouting.

But this time she could get no more than a qualified promise
out of me. To tell the truth, I would have wagered a handsome
sum that the story of my expedition that summer would stain no
paper and spoil not a single pen. And that shows how little we
know what the future holds, for here I am, fulfilling my qualified
promise and writing, as I never thought to write, a book—though
it will hardly serve as an introduction to political life and has not
a jot to do with the Tyrol.

Neither would it, I fear, please Lady Burlesdon if I were to sub-
mit it to her critical eye—a step which I have no intention of taking.

2

Concerning the Colour of Men's Hair

It was a maxim of my Uncle William's that no man should pass
through Paris without spending four-and-twenty hours there. My
uncle spoke out of a ripe experience of the world, and I honoured
his advice by putting up for a day and a night at The Continental
on my way to the Tyrol. I called on George Featherly at the embassy, and we had a bit of dinner together at Durand's and afterwards dropped in to the opera, and after that we had a little supper, and after that we called on Bertram Bertrand, a versifier of
some repute and Paris correspondent to *The Critic*. He had a very
comfortable suite of rooms, and we found some pleasant fellows
smoking and talking. It struck me, however, that Bertram himself
was absent and in low spirits, and when everybody except ourselves had gone I rallied him on his moping preoccupation. He
fenced with me for a while, but at last, flinging himself on a sofa,
he exclaimed, "Very well. Have it your own way. I am in love—
infernally in love!"

"Oh, you'll write the better poetry," said I by way of consolation.

He ruffled his hair with his hand and smoked furiously. George
Featherly, standing with his back to the mantelpiece, smiled un-
kindly.

"If it's the old affair," said he, "you may as well throw it up,
Bert. She's leaving Paris tomorrow."

"I know that," snapped Bertram.

"Not that it would make any difference if she stayed," pursued
the relentless George. "She flies higher than the paper trade, my
boy!"

"Hang her!" said Bertram.

"It would make it more interesting for me," I ventured to observe, "if I knew who you were talking about."

"Antoinette Mauban," said George.

"De Mauban," growled Bertram.

"Oho!" said I, passing by the question of the de. "You don't mean to say, Bert—"

"Can't you let me alone?"

"Where's she going to?" I asked, for the lady was something of a celebrity.

George jingled his money, smiled cruelly at poor Bertram, and answered pleasantly, "Nobody knows. By the way, Bert, I met a great man at her house the other night—at least, about a month ago. Did you ever meet him—the Duke of Strelsau?"

"Yes, I did," growled Bertram.

"An extremely accomplished man, I thought him."

It was not hard to see that George's references to the duke were intended to aggravate poor Bertram's sufferings, so that I drew the inference that the duke had distinguished Mme de Mauban by his attentions. She was a widow, rich, handsome, and, according to repute, ambitious. It was quite possible that she, as George put it, was flying as high as a personage who was everything he could be short of enjoying a strictly royal rank, for the duke was the son of the late King of Ruritania by a second and morganatic marriage, and half brother to the new king. He had been his father's favourite, and it had occasioned some unfavourable comment when he had been created a duke with a title derived from no less a city than the capital itself. His mother had been of good, but not exalted, birth.

"He's not in Paris now, is he?" I asked.

"Oh, no! He's gone back to be present at the king's coronation; a ceremony which, I should say, he'll not enjoy much. But, Bert, old man, don't despair! He won't marry the fair Antoinette—at least, not unless another plan comes to nothing. Still, perhaps, she—" He paused and added with a laugh, "Royal attentions are hard to resist—you know that, don't you, Rudolf?"

"Confound you!" said I, and, rising, I left the hapless Bertram in George's hands and went home to bed.

The next day George Featherly went with me to the station, where I took a ticket for Dresden.

"Going to see the pictures?" asked George, with a grin.

George is an inveterate gossip, and had I told him that I was off to Ruritania the news would have been in London in three days and in Park Lane in a week. I was therefore about to return an evasive answer when he saved my conscience by leaving me suddenly and darting across the platform. Following him with my eyes, I saw him lift his hat and accost a graceful, fashionably dressed woman who had just appeared from the booking office. She was perhaps a year or two over thirty, tall, dark, and of rather full figure. As George talked, I saw her glance at me, and my vanity was hurt by the thought that, muffled in a fur coat and a neck wrapper (for it was a chilly April day) and wearing a soft travelling hat pulled down to my ears, I must be looking very far from my best. A moment later George rejoined me.

"You've got a charming travelling companion," he said. "That's poor Bert Bertrand's goddess, Antoinette de Mauban, and, like you, she's going to Dresden—also, no doubt, to see the pictures. It's very queer, though, that she doesn't at present desire the honour of your acquaintance."

"I didn't ask to be introduced," I observed, a little annoyed.

"Well, I offered to bring you to her, but she said, 'Another time.' Never mind, old fellow, perhaps there'll be a smash, and you'll have a chance of rescuing her and cutting out the Duke of Strelsau!"

No smash, however, happened, either to me or to Mme de Mauban. I can speak for her as confidently as for myself, for when, after a night's rest in Dresden, I continued my journey she got into the same train. Understanding that she wished to be let alone, I avoided her carefully, but I saw that she went the same way as I did to the very end of my journey, and I took opportunities of having a good look at her when I could do so unobserved.

As soon as we reached the Ruritanian frontier (where the old officer who presided over the custom house favoured me with such a stare that I felt surer than before of my Elphberg physiognomy) I bought the papers and found in them news which affected my movements. For some reason, which was not clearly explained and seemed to be something of a mystery, the date of the coronation had been suddenly advanced, and the ceremony was to take place on the next day but one. The whole country seemed in a stir about it, and it was evident that Strelsau was thronged. Rooms were all let and hotels overflowing. There would be very little chance of my obtaining a lodging, and I should certainly have to pay an exorbitant charge for it. I made up my mind to stop at Zenda, a small town fifty miles short of the capital and about ten from the frontier. My train reached there in the evening. I would spend the next day, Tuesday, in a wander over the hills, which were said to be very fine, and in taking a glance at the famous castle, and go over by train to Strelsau on the Wednesday morning, returning at night to sleep at Zenda.

Accordingly, at Zenda I got out, and as the train passed where I stood on the platform, I saw my friend Mme de Mauban in her place. Clearly she was going through to Strelsau, having, with more providence than I could boast, secured apartments there. I smiled to think how surprised George Featherly would have been to know that she and I had been fellow-travellers for so long.

I was very kindly received at the hotel—it was really no more than an inn—kept by a fat old lady and her two daughters. They were good, quiet people and seemed very little interested in the great doings at Strelsau. The old lady's hero was the duke, for he was now, under the late king's will, master of the Zenda estates and of the castle, which rose grandly on its steep hill at the end of the valley, a mile or so from the inn. The old lady, indeed, did not hesitate to express regret that the duke was not on the throne instead of his brother.

"We know Duke Michael," said she. "He has always lived among us. Every Ruritanian knows Duke Michael. But the king is almost a stranger. He has been so much abroad not one in ten knows him even by sight."

"And now," chimed in one of the young women, "they say he has shaved off his beard, so that no one at all knows him."

"Shaved his beard!" exclaimed her mother. "Who says so?"

"Johann, the duke's keeper. He has seen the king."

"Ah, yes. The king, sir, is now at the duke's shooting lodge in the forest here. From here he goes to Strelsau to be crowned on Wednesday morning."

I was interested to hear this and made up my mind to walk next day in the direction of the lodge on the chance of coming across the king. The old lady ran on garrulously, "Ah! And I wish he would stay at his shooting—that and wine (and one thing more) are all he loves, they say—and suffer our duke to be crowned on Wednesday. That I wish, and I don't care who knows it."

"Hush, mother!" urged the daughters.

"Oh, there's many to think as I do!" cried the old woman stubbornly.

I threw myself back in my deep armchair and laughed at her zeal.

"For my part," said the younger and prettier of the two daughters, a fair, buxom, smiling wench, "I hate Black Michael! A real Elphberg for me, mother! The king, they say, is as red as a fox or as—"

And she laughed mischievously as she cast a glance at me and tossed her head at her sister's reproving face.

"Many a man has cursed this red hair before now," muttered the old lady—and I remembered James, fifth Earl of Burlesdon.

"But never a woman!" cried the girl.

"Aye, and women, when it was too late," was the stern answer, reducing the girl to silence and blushes.

"How comes the king here?" I asked, to break an embarrassed silence. "It is the duke's land here, you say."

"The duke invited him, sir, to rest here till Wednesday. The duke is at Strelsau, preparing the king's reception."

"Then they're friends?"

"None better," said the old lady.

But my rosy damsel tossed her head again. She was not to be repressed for long, and she broke out again, "Aye, they love one another as men do who want the same place and the same wife!"

The old woman glowered, but the last words pricked my curiosity, and I interposed before she could begin scolding, "What, the same wife, too! How's that, young lady?"

"All the world knows that Black Michael—well, then, mother, the duke—would give his soul to marry his cousin, the Princess Flavia, and that she is to be the queen."

"Upon my word," said I, "I begin to be sorry for your duke. But if a man will be a younger son, why, he must take what the elder leaves and be as thankful to God as he can," and, thinking of myself, I shrugged my shoulders and laughed. And then I thought also of Antoinette de Mauban and her journey to Strelsau.

"It's little dealing Black Michael has with—" began the girl, braving her mother's anger, but as she spoke a heavy step sounded on the floor, and a gruff voice asked in a threatening tone, "Who talks of 'Black Michael' in his Highness' own burgh?"

The girl gave a little shriek, half of fright—half, I think, of amusement.

"You'll not tell of me, Johann?" she said.

"See where your chatter leads," said the old lady.

The man who had spoken came forward.

"We have company, Johann," said my hostess, and the fellow plucked off his cap. A moment later he saw me, and to my amazement he started back a step as though he had seen something wonderful.

"What ails you, Johann?" asked the elder girl. "This is a gentleman on his travels, come to see the coronation."

The man had recovered himself, but he was staring at me with an intense, searching, almost fierce glance.

"Good evening to you," said I.

"Good evening, sir," he muttered, still scrutinizing me, and the merry girl began to laugh as she called, "See, Johann, it is the colour you love! He started to see your hair, sir. It's not the colour we see most of here in Zenda."

"I crave your pardon, sir," stammered the fellow, with puzzled eyes. "I expected to see no one."

"Give him a glass to drink my health in, and I'll bid you good night, and thanks to you, ladies, for your courtesy and pleasant conversation."

So speaking, I rose to my feet and with a slight bow turned to the door. The young girl ran to light me on the way, and the man fell back to let me pass, his eyes still fixed on me. The moment I was by he started a step forward, asking, "Pray, sir, do you know our king?"

"I never saw him," said I. "I hope to do so on Wednesday."

He said no more, but I felt his eyes following me till the door closed behind me. My saucy conductor, looking over her shoulder at me as she preceded me upstairs, said, "There's no pleasing Master Johann for one of your colour, sir."

"He prefers yours, maybe?" I suggested.

"I meant, sir, in a man," she answered, with a coquettish glance.

"What," asked I, taking hold of the other side of the candlestick, "does colour matter in a man?"

"Nay, but I love yours—it's the Elphberg red."

"Colour in a man," said I, "is a matter of no more moment than that!" and I gave her something of no value.

"God send the kitchen door be shut!" said she.

"Amen!" said I, and left her.

In fact, however, as I now know, colour is sometimes of considerable moment to a man.

3

A Merry Evening with a Distant Relative

I was not so unreasonable as to be prejudiced against the duke's keeper because he disliked my complexion, and if I had been, his most civil and obliging conduct (as it seemed to me to be) next morning would have disarmed me. Hearing that I was bound for Strelsau, he came to see me while I was breakfasting and told me that a sister of his, who had married a well-to-do tradesman and lived in the capital, had invited him to occupy a room in her house. He had gladly accepted but now found that his duties would not permit of his absence. He begged, therefore, that if such humble (though, as he added, clean and comfortable) lodgings would satisfy me I would take his place. He pledged his sister's acquiescence, and urged the inconvenience and crowding to which I should be subject in my journeys to and from Strelsau the next day. I accepted his offer without a moment's hesitation, and he went off to telegraph to his sister while I packed up and prepared to take the next train. But I still hankered after the forest and the shooting lodge, and when my little maid told me that I could, by walking ten miles or so through the forest, hit the railway at a roadside station, I decided to send my luggage direct to the address which Johann had given, take my walk, and follow to Strelsau myself. Johann had gone off and was not aware of the change in my plans, but as its only effect was to delay my arrival at his sister's for a few hours, there was no reason for troubling to inform him of it. Doubtless the good lady would waste no anxiety on my account.

I took an early luncheon, and having bidden my kind entertainers farewell, promising to return to them on my way home, I set out to climb the hill that led to the castle and thence to the forest of Zenda. Half an hour's leisurely walking brought me to the castle. It had been a fortress in old days, and the ancient keep was still in good preservation and very imposing. Behind it stood another portion of the original castle, and behind that again, and separated from it by a deep and broad moat, which ran all round the old buildings, was a handsome modern chateau, erected by the last king and now forming the country residence of the Duke of Strelsau. The old and the new portions were connected by a drawbridge, and this indirect mode of access formed the only passage between the old building and the outer world, but leading to the modern chateau there was a broad and handsome avenue. It was an ideal residence. When "Black Michael" desired company he could dwell in his chateau. If a fit of misanthropy seized him he had merely to cross the bridge and draw it up after him (it ran on rollers), and nothing short of a regiment and a train of artillery could fetch him out. I went on my way, glad that poor Black Michael, though he could not have the throne or the princess, had at least got as fine a residence as any prince in Europe.

Soon I entered the forest and walked on for an hour or more in its cool, sombre shade. The great trees enlaced with one another over my head, and the sunshine stole through in patches as bright as diamonds, and hardly bigger. I was enchanted with the place, and finding a felled tree trunk, propped my back against it, and stretching my legs out, gave myself up to undisturbed contemplation of the solemn beauty of the woods and to the comfort of a good cigar. And when the cigar was finished, and I had (I suppose) inhaled as much beauty as I could, I went off into the most delightful sleep, regardless of my train to Strelsau and of the fast-waning afternoon. To remember a train in such a spot would have been rank sacrilege. Instead of that I fell to dreaming that I was married to the Princess Flavia and dwelt in the castle of Zenda, and beguiled whole days with my love in the glades of the forest, which made a very pleasant dream. In fact, I was just impressing a fervent kiss on the charming lips of the princess when I heard (and the voice seemed at first a part of the dream) someone exclaim in rough, strident tones, "Why, the devil's in it! Shave him and he'd be the king!"

The idea seemed whimsical enough for a dream. By the sacrifice of my heavy moustache and carefully pointed imperial I was to be transformed into a monarch! I was about to kiss the princess again when I arrived (very reluctantly) at the conclusion that I was awake.

I opened my eyes and found two men regarding me with much curiosity. Both wore shooting costumes and carried guns. One was rather short and very stoutly built, with a big bullet-shaped head, a bristly grey moustache, and small pale-blue eyes, a trifle bloodshot. The other was a slender young fellow of middle height, dark in complexion, and bearing himself with grace and distinction. I set the one down as an old soldier, the other for a gentleman accustomed to move in good society but not unused to military life either. It turned out afterwards that my guess was a good one.

The elder man approached me, beckoning the younger to follow. He did so, courteously raising his hat. I rose slowly to my feet.

"He's the height, too!" I heard the elder murmur as he surveyed my six feet two inches of stature. Then, with a cavalier touch of the cap, he addressed me, "May I ask your name?"

"As you have taken the first step in the acquaintance, gentlemen," said I, with a smile, "suppose you give me a lead in the matter of names."

The young man stepped forward with a pleasant smile.

"This," said he, "is Colonel Sapt, and I am called Fritz von Tarlenheim. We are both in the service of the King of Ruritania."

I bowed and, baring my head, answered, "I am Rudolf Rassendyll. I am a traveller from England, and once for a year or two I held a commission from her Majesty the Queen."

"Then we are all brethren of the sword," answered Tarlenheim, holding out his hand, which I took readily.

"Rassendyll, Rassendyll!" muttered Colonel Sapt, then a gleam of intelligence flitted across his face.

"By Heaven!" he cried, "you're of the Burlesdons?"

"My brother is now Lord Burlesdon," said I.

"Thy head betrayeth thee," he chuckled, pointing to my uncovered poll. "Why, Fritz, you know the story?"

The young man glanced apologetically at me. He felt a delicacy which my sister-in-law would have admired. To put him at his ease I remarked, with a smile, "Ah! The story is known here as well as among us, it seems."

"Known!" cried Sapt. "If you stay here the deuce a man in all Ruritania will doubt of it—or a woman either."

I began to feel uncomfortable. Had I realized what a very plainly written pedigree I carried about with me I should have thought long before I visited Ruritania. However, I was in for it now.

At this moment a ringing voice sounded from the wood behind us, "Fritz, Fritz! Where are you, man?"

Tarlenheim started, and said hastily, "It's the king!"

Old Sapt chuckled again.

Then a young man jumped out from behind the trunk of a tree and stood beside us. As I looked on him I uttered an astonished cry, and he, seeing me, drew back in sudden wonder. Saving the hair on my face and a manner of conscious dignity which his position gave him, saving also that he lacked perhaps half an inch—nay, less than that, but still something—of my height, the king of Ruritania might have been Rudolf Rassendyll, and I Rudolf the King.

For an instant we stood motionless, looking at one another. Then I bared my head again and bowed respectfully. The king found his voice, and asked in bewilderment, "Colonel—Fritz—who is this gentleman?"

I was about to answer when Colonel Sapt stepped between the king and me, and began to talk to his Majesty in a low growl. The king towered over Sapt, and as he listened his eyes now and again sought mine. I looked at him long and carefully. The likeness was certainly astonishing, though I saw the points of difference also. The king's face was slightly more fleshy than mine, the oval of its contour the least trifle more pronounced, and, as I fancied, his mouth lacking something of the firmness (or obstinacy) which was to be gathered from my close-shutting lips. But for all that, and above all minor distinctions, the likeness rose striking, salient, wonderful.

Sapt ceased speaking, and the king still frowned. Then, gradually, the corners of his mouth began to twitch, his nose came down (as mine does when I laugh), his eyes twinkled, and, behold! he burst into the merriest fit of irrepressible laughter, which rang through the woods and proclaimed him a jovial soul.

"Well met, cousin!" he cried, stepping up to me, clapping me on the back, and laughing still. "You must forgive me if I was taken aback. A man doesn't expect to see double at this time of day, eh, Fritz?"

"I must pray pardon, sire, for my presumption," said I. "I trust it will not forfeit your Majesty's favour."

"By Heaven! You'll always enjoy the king's countenance," he laughed, "whether I like it or not; and, sir, I shall very gladly add to it what services I can. Where are you travelling to?"

"To Strelsau, sire—to the coronation."

The king looked at his friends. He still smiled, though his expression hinted some uneasiness. But the humorous side of the matter caught him again.

"Fritz, Fritz!" he cried, "a thousand crowns for a sight of brother Michael's face when he sees a pair of us!" and the merry laugh rang out again.

"Seriously," observed Fritz von Tarlenheim, "I question Mr Rassendyll's wisdom in visiting Strelsau just now."

The king lit a cigarette.

"Well, Sapt?" said he questioningly.

"He mustn't go," growled the old fellow.

"Come, colonel, you mean that I should be in Mr Rassendyll's debt if—"

"Oh, aye! Wrap it up in the right way," said Sapt, hauling a great pipe out of his pocket.

"Enough, sire," said I. "I'll leave Ruritania today."

"Now, by thunder, you shan't—and that's sans phrase, as Sapt likes it. For you shall dine with me tonight, happen what will afterwards. Come, man, you don't meet a new relation every day!"

"We dine sparingly tonight," said Fritz von Tarlenheim.

"Not we—with our new cousin for a guest!" cried the king, and as Fritz shrugged his shoulders, he added: "Oh! I'll remember our early start, Fritz."

"So will I—tomorrow morning," said old Sapt, pulling at his pipe.

"Oh, wise old Sapt!" cried the king. "Come, Mr Rassendyll— by the way, what name did they give you?"

"Your Majesty's," I answered, bowing.

"Well, that shows they weren't ashamed of us," he laughed. "Come then, cousin Rudolf. I've got no house of my own here, but my dear brother Michael lends us a place of his, and we'll make shift to entertain you there," and he put his arm through mine, and signing to the others to accompany us, walked me off, westerly, through the forest.

We walked for more than half an hour, and the king smoked cigarettes and chattered incessantly. He was full of interest in my family, laughed heartily when I told him of the portraits with Elphberg hair in our galleries, and yet more heartily when he heard that my expedition to Ruritania was a secret one.

"You have to visit your disreputable cousin on the sly, have you?" said he.

Suddenly emerging from the wood, we came on a small and rude shooting lodge. It was a one-storey building, a sort of bunga- low, built entirely of wood. As we approached it a little man in a plain livery came out to meet us. The only other person I saw about the place was a fat elderly woman, whom I afterwards dis- covered to be the mother of Johann, the duke's keeper.

"Well, is dinner ready, Josef?" asked the king.

The little servant informed us that it was, and we soon sat down to a plentiful meal. The fare was plain enough. The king ate heart- ily, Fritz von Tarlenheim delicately, old Sapt voraciously. I plied a good knife and fork, as my custom is. The king noticed my per- formance with approval.

"We're all good trenchermen, we Elphbergs," said he. "But what?—We're eating dry! Wine, Josef! Wine, man! Are we beasts, to eat without drinking? Are we cattle, Josef?"

At this reproof Josef hastened to load the table with bottles.

"Remember tomorrow!" said Fritz.

"Aye—tomorrow!" said old Sapt.

The king drained a bumper to his "Cousin Rudolf", as he was gracious—or merry—enough to call me, and I drank its fellow to the "Elphberg red," whereat he laughed loudly.

No, be the meat what it might, the wine we drank was beyond all price or praise, and we did it justice. Fritz ventured once to stay the king's hand.

"What?" cried the king. "Remember you start before I do, Master Fritz—you must be more sparing by two hours than I."

Fritz saw that I did not understand.

"The colonel and I," he explained, "leave here at six. We ride down to Zenda and return with the guard of honour to fetch the king at eight, and then we all ride together to the station."

"Hang that same guard!" growled Sapt.

"Oh! It's very civil of my brother to ask the honour for his regiment," said the king. "Come, cousin, you need not start early. Another bottle, man!"

I had another bottle—or, rather, a part of one, for the larger half travelled quickly down his Majesty's throat. Fritz gave up his attempts at persuasion. From persuading he fell to being persuaded, and soon we were all of us as full of wine as we had any right to be. The king began talking of what he would do in the future, old Sapt of what he had done in the past, Fritz of some beautiful girl or other, and I of the wonderful merits of the Elphberg dynasty. We all talked at once, and followed to the letter Sapt's exhortation to let the morrow take care of itself.

At last the king set down his glass and leaned back in his chair.

"I have drunk enough," said he.

"Far be it from me to contradict the king," said I.

Indeed, his remark was most absolutely true—so far as it went.

While I yet spoke, Josef came and set before the king a marvellous old wicker-covered flagon. It had lain so long in some darkened cellar that it seemed to blink in the candlelight.

"His Highness the Duke of Strelsau bade me set this wine before the king when the king was weary of all other wines and pray the king to drink for the love that he bears his brother."

"Well done, Black Michael!" said the king. "Out with the cork, Josef. Hang him! Did he think I'd flinch from his bottle?"

The bottle was opened, and Josef filled the king's glass. The king tasted it. Then, with a solemnity born of the hour and his own condition, he looked round on us.

"Gentlemen, my friends—Rudolf, my cousin ('tis a scandalous story, Rudolf, on my honour!)—everything is yours to the half of Ruritania. But ask me not for a single drop of this divine bottle, which I will drink to the health of that—that sly knave, my brother, Black Michael."

And the king seized the bottle and turned it over his mouth, and drained it and flung it from him, and laid his head on his arms on the table.

And we drank pleasant dreams to his Majesty—and that is all I remember of the evening. Perhaps it is enough.

4

The King keeps his Appointment

Whether I had slept a minute or a year I knew not. I awoke with a start and a shiver; my face, hair, and clothes dripped water, and opposite me stood old Sapt, a sneering smile on his face and an empty bucket in his hand. On the table by him sat Fritz von Tarlenheim, pale as a ghost and black as a crow under the eyes.

I leaped to my feet in anger.

"Your joke goes too far, sir!" I cried.

"Tut, man, we've no time for quarrelling. Nothing else would rouse you. It's five o'clock."

"I'll thank you, Colonel Sapt—" I began again, hot in spirit though I was uncommonly cold in body.

"Rassendyll," interrupted Fritz, getting down from the table and taking my arm, "look here."

The king lay full length on the floor. His face was red as his hair, and he breathed heavily. Sapt, the disrespectful old dog, kicked him sharply. He did not stir, nor was there any break in his breathing. I saw that his face and head were wet with water, as were mine.

"We've spent half an hour on him," said Fritz.

"He drank three times what either of you did," growled Sapt.

I knelt down and felt his pulse. It was alarmingly languid and slow. We three looked at one another.

"Was it drugged—that last bottle?" I asked in a whisper.

"I don't know," said Sapt.

"We must get a doctor."

"There's none within ten miles, and a thousand doctors

wouldn't take him to Strelsau today. I know the look of it. He'll not move for six or seven hours yet."

"But the coronation!" I cried in horror.

Fritz shrugged his shoulders, as I began to see was his habit on most occasions.

"We must send word that he's ill," he said.

"I suppose so," said I.

Old Sapt, who seemed as fresh as a daisy, had lit his pipe and was puffing hard at it.

"If he's not crowned today," said he, "I'll lay a crown he's never crowned."

"But, Heavens, why?"

"The whole nation's there to meet him; half the army—aye, and Black Michael at the head. Shall we send word that the king's drunk?"

"That he's ill," said I, in correction.

"Ill!" echoed Sapt, with a scornful laugh. "They know his illnesses too well. He's been 'ill' before!"

"Well, we must chance what they think," said Fritz helplessly. "I'll carry the news and make the best of it."

Sapt raised his hand.

"Tell me," said he, "do you think the king was drugged?"

"I do," said I.

"And who drugged him?"

"That damned hound, Black Michael," said Fritz between his teeth.

"Aye," said Sapt, "that he might not come to be crowned. Rassendyll here doesn't know our pretty Michael. What think you, Fritz—has Michael no king ready? Has half Strelsau no other candidate? As God's alive, man, the throne's lost if the king show himself not in Strelsau today. I know Black Michael."

"We could carry him there," said I.

"And a very pretty picture he makes," sneered Sapt.

Fritz von Tarlenheim buried his face in his hands. The king breathed loudly and heavily. Sapt stirred him again with his foot.

"The drunken dog!" he said. "But he's an Elphberg and the son of his father, and may I rot in hell before Black Michael sits in his place!"

For a moment or two we were all silent. Then Sapt, knitting his bushy grey brows, took his pipe from his mouth and said to me, "As a man grows old he believes in Fate. Fate sent you here. Fate sends you now to Strelsau."

I staggered back, murmuring, "Good God!"

Fritz looked up with an eager, bewildered gaze.

"Impossible!" I muttered. "I should be known."

"It's a risk—against a certainty," said Sapt. "If you shave I'll wager you'll not be known. Are you afraid?"

"Sir!"

"Come, lad, there, there; but it's your life, you know, if you're known—and mine—and Fritz's here. But if you don't go I swear to you Black Michael will sit tonight on the throne, and the king lie in prison or his grave."

"The king would never forgive it," I stammered.

"Are we women? Who cares for his forgiveness?"

The clock ticked fifty times, and sixty and seventy times, as I stood in thought. Then I suppose a look came over my face, for old Sapt caught me by the hand, crying, "You'll go?"

"Yes, I'll go," said I, and I turned my eyes on the prostrate figure of the king on the floor.

"Tonight," Sapt went on in a hasty whisper, "we are to lodge in the palace. The moment they leave us, you and I will mount our horses—Fritz must stay here and guard the king's room—and ride here at a gallop. The king will be ready—Josef will tell him—and he must ride back with me to Strelsau, and you ride as if the devil were behind you to the frontier."

I took it all in in a second and nodded my head.

"There's a chance," said Fritz, with his first sign of hopefulness.

"If I escape detection," said I.

"If we're detected," said Sapt, "I'll send Black Michael down below before I go myself, so help me Heaven! Sit in that chair, man."

I obeyed him.

He darted from the room, calling, "Josef! Josef!" In three minutes he was back, and Josef with him. The latter carried a jug of hot water, soap, and razors. He was trembling as Sapt told him how the land lay and bade him shave me.

Suddenly Fritz smote on his thigh. "But the guard! They'll know! They'll know!"

"Pooh! We shan't wait for the guard. We'll ride to Hofban and catch a train there. When they come the bird'll be flown."

"But the king?"

"The king will be in the wine cellar. I'm going to carry him there now."

"If they find him?"

"They won't. How should they? Josef will put them off."

"But—"

Sapt stamped his foot. "We're not playing," he roared. "My God! Don't I know the risk? If they do find him he's no worse off than if he isn't crowned today in Strelsau."

So speaking, he flung the door open and, stooping, put forth a strength I did not dream he had and lifted the king in his hands. And as he did so, the old woman, Johann the keeper's mother, stood in the doorway. For a moment she stood, then she turned on her heel without a sign of surprise and clattered down the passage.

"Has she heard?" cried Fritz.

"I'll shut her mouth!" said Sapt grimly, and he bore off the king in his arms.

For me, I sat down in an armchair, and as I sat there, half dazed, Josef clipped and scraped me till my moustache and imperial were things of the past and my face was as bare as the king's. And when Fritz saw me thus he drew a long breath and exclaimed, "By Jove, we shall do it!"

It was six o'clock now, and we had no time to lose. Sapt hurried me into the king's room, and I dressed myself in the uniform of a colonel of the Guard, finding time as I slipped on the king's boots to ask Sapt what he had done with the old woman.

"She swore she'd heard nothing," said he, "but to make sure I tied her legs together and put a handkerchief in her mouth and bound her hands, and locked her up in the coal cellar, next door to the king. Josef'll look after them both later on."

Then I burst out laughing, and even old Sapt grimly smiled.

"I fancy," said he, "that when Josef tells them the king is gone they'll think it is because we smelt a rat. For you may swear Black Michael doesn't expect to see him in Strelsau today."

I put the king's helmet on my head. Old Sapt handed me the king's sword, looking at me long and carefully.

"Thank God, he shaved his beard!" he exclaimed.

"Why did he?" I asked.

"Because Princess Flavia said he grazed her cheek when he was graciously pleased to give her a cousinly kiss. Come, though, we must ride."

"Is all safe here?"

"Nothing's safe anywhere," said Sapt, "but we can make it no safer."

Fritz now rejoined us in the uniform of a captain in the same regiment as that to which my dress belonged. In four minutes Sapt had arrayed himself in his uniform. Josef called that the horses were ready. We jumped on their backs and started at a rapid trot. The game had begun. What would the issue of it be?

The cool morning air cleared my head, and I was able to take in all Sapt said to me. He was wonderful. Fritz hardly spoke, riding like a man asleep, but Sapt, without another word for the king, began at once to instruct me most minutely in the history of my past life, of my family, of my tastes, pursuits, weaknesses, friends, companions, and servants. He told me the etiquette of the Ruritanian court, promising to be constantly at my elbow to point out everybody whom I ought to know and give me hints with what degree of favour to greet them.

"By the way," he said, "you are a Catholic, I suppose?"

"Not I," I answered.

"Lord, he's a heretic!" groaned Sapt, and forthwith he fell to a rudimentary lesson in the practices and observances of the Romish faith.

"Luckily," said he, "you won't be expected to know much, for the king's notoriously lax and careless about such matters. But you must be as civil as butter to the cardinal. We hope to win him over because he and Michael have a standing quarrel about their precedence." ·

We were by now at the station. Fritz had recovered nerve enough to explain to the astonished station master that the king had changed his plans. The train steamed up. We got into a first-class carriage, and Sapt, leaning back on the cushions, went on with his lesson. I looked at my watch—the king's watch it was, of course. It was just eight.

"I wonder if they've gone to look for us," I said.

"I hope they won't find the king," said Fritz nervously, and this time it was Sapt who shrugged his shoulders.

The train travelled well, and at half-past nine, looking out of the window, I saw the towers and spires of a great city.

"Your capital, my liege," grinned old Sapt with a wave of his hand, and, leaning forwards, he laid his finger on my pulse. "A little too quick," said he in his grumbling tone.

"I'm not made of stone!" I exclaimed.

"You'll do," said he with a nod. "We must say Fritz has caught the ague. Drain your flask, Fritz, for Heaven's sake, boy!"

Fritz did as he was bid.

"We're an hour early," said Sapt. "We'll send word forwards of your Majesty's arrival, for there'll be no one here to meet us yet. And meanwhile—"

"Meanwhile," said I, "the king'll be hanged if he doesn't have some breakfast."

Old Sapt chuckled, and held out his hand.

"You're an Elphberg, every inch of you," said he. Then he paused, and looking at us, said quietly, "God send we may be alive tonight!"

"Amen!" said Fritz von Tarlenheim.

The train stopped. Fritz and Sapt leaped out, uncovered, and held the door for me. I choked down a lump that rose in my throat, settled my helmet firmly on my head, and (I'm not ashamed to say it) breathed a short prayer to God. Then I stepped on the platform of the station at Strelsau.

A moment later all was bustle and confusion: men hurrying up, hats in hand, and hurrying off again; men conducting me to the buffet; men mounting and riding in hot haste to the quarters of the troops, to the cathedral, to the residence of Duke Michael. Even as I swallowed the last drop of my cup of coffee the bells throughout all the city broke out into a joyful peal, and the sound of a military band and of men cheering smote upon my ear.

King Rudolf the Fifth was in his good city of Strelsau! And they shouted outside, "God save the king!"

Old Sapt's mouth wrinkled into a smile.

"God save 'em both!" he whispered. "Courage, lad!" and I felt his hand press my knee.

5

The Adventures of an Understudy

With Fritz von Tarlenheim and Colonel Sapt close behind me, I stepped out of the buffet on to the platform. The last thing I did was to feel if my revolver were handy and my sword loose in the scabbard. A colourful group of officers and high dignitaries stood awaiting me, at their head a tall old man, covered with medals, and of military bearing. He wore the yellow and red ribbon of the Red Rose of Ruritania—which, by the way, decorated my unworthy breast also.

"Marshal Strakencz," whispered Sapt, and I knew that I was in the presence of the most famous veteran of the Ruritanian army.

Just behind the marshal stood a short, spare man in flowing robes of black and crimson.

"The chancellor of the kingdom," whispered Sapt.

The marshal greeted me in a few loyal words and proceeded to deliver an apology from the Duke of Strelsau. The duke, it seemed, had been afflicted with a sudden indisposition which made it impossible for him to come to the station, but he craved leave to await his Majesty at the cathedral. I expressed my concern, accepted the marshal's excuses very suavely, and received the compliments of a large number of distinguished personages. No one betrayed the least suspicion, and I felt my nerve returning and the agitated beating of my heart subsiding. But Fritz was still pale, and his hand shook like a leaf as he extended it to the marshal.

Presently we formed procession and took our way to the door of the station. Here I mounted my horse, the marshal holding my stirrup. The civil dignitaries went off to their carriages, and I started to ride through the streets with the marshal on my right and Sapt (who, as my chief aide-de-camp, was entitled to the place) on my left. The city of Strelsau is partly old and partly new. Spacious modern boulevards and residential quarters surround and embrace the narrow, tortuous and picturesque streets of the original town. In the outer circles the upper classes live; in the inner the shops are situated; and behind their prosperous fronts lie hidden populous but wretched lanes and alleys, filled with a poverty-stricken, turbulent and (in large measure) criminal class. These social and local divisions corresponded, as I knew from Sapt's information, to another division more important to me. The New Town was for the king, but to the Old Town Michael of Strelsau was a hope, a hero, and a darling.

The scene was very brilliant as we passed along the Grand Boulevard and on to the great square where the royal palace stood. Here I was in the midst of my devoted adherents. Every house was hung with red and bedecked with flags and mottoes. The streets were lined with raised seats on each side, and I passed along, bowing this way and that, under a shower of cheers, blessings, and waving handkerchiefs. The balconies were full of gaily dressed ladies, who clapped their hands and curtsied and threw their brightest glances at me. A torrent of red roses fell on me. One bloom lodged in my horse's mane, and I took it and stuck it in my coat. The marshal smiled grimly. I had stolen some glances at his face, but he was too impassive to show me whether his sympathies were with me or not.

"The red rose for the Elphbergs, marshal," said I gaily, and he nodded.

I have written "gaily", and a strange word it must seem. But the truth is that I was drunk with excitement. At that moment I believed—I almost believed—that I was in very truth the king, and with a look of laughing triumph I raised my eyes to the beauty-laden balconies again . . . and then I started. For looking down on me, with her handsome face and proud smile, was the lady who had been my fellow traveller—Antoinette de Mauban—and I saw her also start, and her lips moved, and she leaned forwards and gazed at me. And I, collecting myself, met her eyes full and square while again I felt my revolver. Suppose she had cried aloud, "That's not the king!"

Well, we went by, and then the marshal, turning round in his saddle, waved his hand, and the cuirassiers closed round us so that the crowd could not come near me. We were leaving my quarter and entering Duke Michael's, and this action of the marshal's showed me more clearly than words what the state of feeling in the town must be. But if Fate made me a king, the least I could do was to play the part handsomely.

"Why this change in our order, marshal?" said I.

The marshal bit his white moustache. "It is more prudent, sire," he murmured.

I drew rein. "Let those in front ride on," said I, "till they are fifty yards ahead. But do you, marshal, and Colonel Sapt and my friends wait here till I have ridden fifty yards. And see that no one is nearer to me. I will have my people see that their king trusts them."

Sapt laid his hand on my arm. I shook him off. The marshal hesitated.

"Am I not understood?" said I, and, biting his moustache again, he gave the orders. I saw old Sapt smiling into his beard, but he shook his head at me. If I had been killed in open day in the streets of Strelsau Sapt's position would have been a difficult one.

Perhaps I ought to say that I was dressed all in white, except my boots. I wore a silver helmet with gilt ornaments, and the broad ribbon of the Rose looked well across my chest. I should be paying a poor compliment to the king if I did not set modesty aside and admit that I made a very fine figure. So the people thought, for when I, riding alone, entered the dingy, sparsely decorated, sombre streets of the Old Town there was first a murmur, then a cheer, and a woman, from a window above a cookshop, cried the old local saying: "If he's red he's right!" whereat I laughed and took off my helmet that she might see that I was of the right colour, and they cheered me again at that.

It was more interesting riding thus alone, for I heard the comments of the crowd.

"He looks paler than his wont," said one.

"You'd look pale if you lived as he did," was the highly disrespectful retort.

"He a bigger man that I thought," said another.

"So he had a good jaw under that beard, after all," commented
a third.

"The pictures of him aren't handsome enough," declared a
pretty girl, taking great care that I should hear. No doubt it was
mere flattery.

But in spite of these signs of approval and interest, the mass of
people received me in silence and with sullen looks, and my dear
brother's portrait ornamented most of the windows—which was
an ironical sort of greeting to the king. I was quite glad that he
had been spared the unpleasant sight. He was a man of quick
temper, and perhaps he would not have taken it so placidly as I
did.

At last we were at the cathedral. Its great grey front, embel-
lished with hundreds of statues and boasting a pair of the finest
oak doors in Europe, rose for the first time before me, and the
sudden sense of my audacity almost overcame me. Everything
was in a mist as I dismounted. I saw the marshal and Sapt dimly,
and dimly the throng of gorgeously robed priests who awaited
me. And my eyes were still dim as I walked up the great nave,
with the pealing of the organ in my ears. I saw nothing of the brilliant throng that filled it. I hardly distinguished the stately figure
of the cardinal as he rose from the archiepiscopal throne to greet
me. Two faces only stood out side by side clearly before my
eyes—the face of a girl, pale and lovely, surmounted by a crown
of the glorious Elphberg hair (for in a woman it is glorious), and
the face of a man whose full-blooded red cheeks, black hair, and
dark, deep eyes told me that at last I was in the presence of my
brother, Black Michael. And when he saw me his red cheeks went
pale all in a moment, and his helmet fell with a clatter on the
floor. Till that moment I believe that he had not realized that the
king was in very truth come to Strelsau.

Of what followed next I remember nothing. I knelt before the
altar, and the cardinal anointed my head. Then I rose to my feet,

and stretched out my hand and took from him the crown of Ruritania and set it on my head, and I swore the old oath of the king, and (if it were a sin may it be forgiven me) I received the Holy Sacrament there before them all. Then the great organ pealed out again, the marshal bade the heralds proclaim me, and Rudolf the Fifth was crowned king; of which imposing ceremony an excellent picture hangs now in my dining room. The portrait of the king is very good.

Then the lady with the pale face and the glorious hair, her train held by two pages, stepped from her place and came to where I stood. And a herald cried: "Her Royal Highness the Princess Flavia!"

She curtsied low, and put her hand under mine and raised my hand and kissed it. And for an instant I thought what I had best do. Then I drew her to me and kissed her twice on the cheek, and she blushed red, and—why, then his Eminence the Cardinal Archbishop slipped in front of Black Michael, and kissed my hand and presented me with a letter from the Pope—the first and last which I have ever received from that exalted quarter!

And then came the Duke of Strelsau. His step trembled, I swear, and he looked to the right and to the left, as a man looks who thinks on flight; and his face was patched with red and white, and his hand shook so that it jumped under mine, and I felt his lips dry and parched. And I glanced at Sapt, who was smiling again into his beard, and, resolutely doing my duty in that station of life to which I had been marvellously called, I took my dear Michael by both hands and kissed him on the cheek. I think we were both glad when that was over!

But neither in the face of the princess nor in that of any other did I see the least doubt or questioning. Yet had I and the king stood side by side they could have told us apart in an instant, or, at least, on a little consideration. But neither they nor anyone else dreamed or imagined that I could be other than the king. So the likeness served, and for an hour I stood there, feeling as weary and blasé as though I had been a king all my life; and everybody kissed my hand, and the ambassadors paid me their respects, among them old Lord Topham, at whose house in Grosvenor

Square I had danced a score of times. Thank Heaven, the old man was as blind as a bat and did not claim my acquaintance.

Then back we went through the streets to the palace, and I heard them cheering Black Michael, but he, Fritz told me, sat biting his nails like a man in a reverie, and even his own friends said that he should have made a braver show. I was in a carriage now, side by side with the Princess Flavia, and a rough fellow cried out: "And when's the wedding?" and as he spoke another struck him in the face, crying, "Long live Duke Michael!" and the princess coloured—it was an admirable tint—and looked straight in front of her.

Now I felt in a difficulty, because I had forgotten to ask Sapt the state of my affections or how far matters had gone between the princess and myself. Frankly, had I been the king the further they had gone the better should I have been pleased. For I am not a slow-blooded man, and I had not kissed Princess Flavia's cheek for nothing. These thoughts passed through my head, but, not being sure of my ground, I said nothing, and in a moment or two the princess, recovering her equanimity, turned to me.

"Do you know, Rudolf," said she, "you look somehow different today?"

The fact was not surprising, but the remark was disquieting.

"You look," she went on, "more sober, more sedate. You're almost careworn, and I declare you're thinner. Surely it's not possible that you've begun to take anything seriously?"

The princess seemed to hold of the king much the same opinion that Lady Burlesdon held of me.

I braced myself up to the conversation. "Would that please you?" I asked softly.

"Oh, you know my views," said she, turning her eyes away.

"Whatever pleases you I try to do," I said, and as I saw her smile and blush I thought that I was playing the king's hand very well for him. So I continued, and what I said was perfectly true: "I assure you, my dear cousin, that nothing in my life has affected me more than the reception I've been greeted with today."

She smiled brightly, but in an instant grew grave again, and whispered, "Did you notice Michael?"

"Yes," said I, adding, "He wasn't enjoying himself."

"Do be careful!" she went on. "You don't—indeed you don't—keep enough watch on him. You know—"

"I know," said I, "that he wants what I've got."

"Yes. Hush!"

Then—and I can't justify it, for I committed the king far beyond what I had a right to do—I suppose she carried me off my feet—I went on, "And, perhaps, also something which I haven't got yet but hope to win some day."

This was my answer—had I been the king I should have thought it encouraging: "Haven't you enough responsibilities on you for one day, cousin?"

Bang, bang! Blare, blare! We were at the palace. Guns were firing and trumpets blowing. Rows of lackeys stood waiting, and, handing the princess up the broad marble staircase, I took formal possession as a crowned king of the house of my ancestors, and sat down at my own table with my cousin on my right hand, on her other side Black Michael, and on my left his Eminence the Cardinal. Behind my chair stood Sapt, and at the end of the table I saw Fritz von Tarlenheim drain to the bottom of his glass of champagne rather sooner than he decently should.

I wondered what the King of Ruritania was doing.

6

The Secret of a Cellar

We were in the king's dressing room—Fritz von Tarlenheim, Sapt, and I. I flung myself exhausted into an armchair. Sapt lit his pipe. He uttered no congratulations on the marvellous success of our wild risk but his whole bearing was eloquent of satisfaction. The triumph, aided perhaps by good wine, had made a new man of Fritz.

"What a day for you to remember!" he cried. "Gad. I'd like to be a king for twelve hours myself! But, Rassendyll, you mustn't throw your heart too much into the part. I don't wonder Black Michael looked blacker than ever—you and the princess had so much to say to one another."

"How beautiful she is!" I exclaimed.

"Never mind the woman," growled Sapt. "Are you ready to start?"

"Yes," said I, with a sigh.

It was five o'clock, and at twelve I should be no more than Rudolf Rassendyll. I remarked on it in a joking tone.

"You'll be lucky," observed Sapt grimly, "if you're not the late Rudolf Rassendyll. By Heaven! I feel my head wobbling on my shoulders every minute you're in the city. Do you know, friend, that Michael has had news from Zenda? He went into a room alone to read it—and he came out looking like a man dazed."

"I'm ready," said I, this news making me none the more eager to linger.

Sapt sat down. "I must write us an order to leave the city. Michael's governor, you know, and we must be prepared for hindrances. You must sign the order."

"My dear colonel, I've not been bred a forger!"

Out of his pocket Sapt produced a piece of paper.

"There's the king's signature," he said, "and here," he went on, after another search in his pocket, "is some tracing paper. If you can't manage a 'Rudolf' in ten minutes, why—I can."

"Your education has been more comprehensive than mine," said I. "You write it."

And a very tolerable forgery did this versatile hero produce.

"Now, Fritz," said he, "the king goes to bed. He is upset. No one is to see him till nine o'clock tomorrow. You understand—no one?"

"I understand," answered Fritz.

"Michael may come and claim immediate audience. You'll answer that only princes of the blood are entitled to it."

"That'll annoy Michael," laughed Fritz.

"You quite understand?" asked Sapt again. "If the door of this room is opened while we're away you're not to be alive to tell us about it."

"I need no schooling, colonel," said Fritz, a trifle haughtily.

"Here, wrap yourself in this big cloak," Sapt continued to me, "and put on this flat cap. My orderly rides with me to the shooting lodge tonight."

"There's an obstacle," I observed. "The horse doesn't live that can carry me forty miles."

"Oh, yes, he does—two of him: one here—one at the lodge. Now, are you ready?"

"I'm ready," said I.

Fritz held out his hand. "In case," said he, and we shook hands heartily.

"Damn your sentiment!" growled Sapt. "Come along."

He went, not to the door but to a panel in the wall.

"In the old king's time," said he, "I knew this way well."

I followed him, and we walked, as I should estimate, near two hundred yards along a narrow passage. Then we came to a stout oak door. Sapt unlocked it. We passed through, and found ourselves in a quiet street that ran along the back of the palace gardens. A man was waiting for us with two horses. One was a mag-

nificent bay, up to any weight; the other a sturdy brown. Sapt
signed to me to mount the bay. Without a word to the man, we
mounted and rode away. The town was full of noise and merri-
ment, but we took secluded ways. My cloak was wrapped over
half my face; the capacious flat cap hid every lock of my telltale
hair. By Sapt's directions I crouched on my saddle and rode with
such a round back as I hope never to exhibit on a horse again.
Down a long, narrow lane we went, meeting some wanderers and
some roisterers; and as we rode we heard the cathedral bells still
clanging out their welcome to the king. It was half-past six, and
still light. At last we came to the city wall and to a gate.

"Have your weapon ready," whispered Sapt. "We must stop his
mouth if he talks."

I put my hand on my revolver. Sapt hailed the doorkeeper. The
stars fought for us! A little girl of fourteen tripped out.

"Please, sir, father's gone to see the king."

"He'd better have stayed here," said Sapt to me, grinning.

"But he said I wasn't to open the gate, sir."

"Did he, my dear?" said Sapt, dismounting. "Then give me the
key."

The key was in the child's hand. Sapt gave her a crown.

"Here's an order from the king. Show it to your father. Orderly,
open the gate!"

I leaped down. Between us we rolled back the great gate, led
our horses out, and closed it again.

"I shall be sorry for the doorkeeper if Michael finds out that he
wasn't there. Now, then, lad, for a canter. We mustn't go too fast
while we're near the town."

Once, however, outside the city we ran little danger, for everybody else was inside, merrymaking, and as the evening fell we
quickened our pace, my splendid horse bounding along under me
as though I had been a feather. It was a fine night, and presently
the moon appeared. We talked little on the way and chiefly about
the progress we were making.

"I wonder what the duke's dispatches told him!" said I, once.

"Aye, I wonder!" responded Sapt.

We stopped for a draught of wine and to bait our horses, losing half an hour thus. I dared not go into the inn and stayed with the horses in the stable. Then we went ahead again and had covered some five-and-twenty miles when Sapt abruptly stopped.

"Hark!" he cried.

I listened. Away, far behind us, in the still of the evening—it was just half-past nine—we heard the beat of horses' hoofs. The wind, blowing strong behind us, carried the sound. I glanced at Sapt.

"Come on!" he cried, and spurred his horse into a gallop. When we next paused to listen the hoof beats were not audible, and we relaxed our pace. Then we heard them again. Sapt jumped down and laid his ear to the ground.

"There are two," he said. "They're only a mile behind. Thank God, the road curves in and out, and the wind's our way."

We galloped on. We seemed to be holding our own. We had entered the outskirts of the forest of Zenda, and the trees, closing in behind us as the track zigged and zagged, prevented us seeing our pursuers and them from seeing us.

Another half an hour brought us to a divide of the road. Sapt drew rein.

"To the right is our road," he said. "To left, to the castle. Each about eight miles. Get down."

"But they'll be on us!" I cried.

"Get down!" he repeated brusquely, and I obeyed.

The wood was dense up to the very edge of the road. We led our horses into the covert, bound handkerchiefs over their eyes, and stood beside them.

"You want to see who they are?" I whispered.

"Aye, and where they're going," he answered.

I saw that his revolver was in his hand.

Nearer and nearer came the hoofs. The moon shone out now clear and full so that the road was white with it. The ground was hard and we had left no traces.

"Here they come!" whispered Sapt.

"It's the duke!"

"I thought so!" he answered.

It was the duke, and with him a burly fellow whom I knew well and who had cause to know me afterwards—Max Holf, brother to Johann the keeper, and body servant to his Highness. They were up to us. The duke reined up. I saw Sapt's finger curl lovingly towards the trigger. I believe he would have given ten years of his life for a shot, and he could have picked off Black Michael as easily as I could a barn-door fowl in a farmyard. I laid my hand on his arm. He nodded reassuringly; he was always ready to sacrifice inclination to duty.

"Which way?" asked Black Michael.

"To the castle, your Highness," urged his companion. "There we shall learn the truth."

For an instant the duke hesitated. "I thought I heard hoofs," said he.

"I think not, your Highness."

"Why shouldn't we go to the lodge?"

"I fear a trap. If all is well why go to the lodge? If not, it's a snare to trap us."

Suddenly the duke's horse neighed. In an instant we folded our cloaks close round our horses' heads, and, holding them thus, covered the duke and his attendant with our revolvers. If they had found us they had been dead men, or our prisoners.

Michael waited a moment longer. Then he cried: "To Zenda, then!" and setting spurs to his horse, galloped on.

Sapt raised his weapon after him, and there was such an expression of wistful regret on his face that I had much ado not to burst out laughing.

For ten minutes we stayed where we were.

"You see," said Sapt, "they've sent him news that all is well."

"What does that mean?" I asked.

"God knows," said Sapt, frowning heavily. "But it's brought him from Strelsau in a rare puzzle."

Then we mounted and rode fast as our weary horses could lay their feet to the ground. For those last eight miles we spoke no more. Our minds were full of apprehension. "All is well." What did it mean? Was all well with the king?

At last the lodge came in sight. Spurring our horses to a last gallop, we rode up to the gate. All was still and quiet. Not a soul came to meet us. We dismounted in haste. Suddenly Sapt caught me by the arm.

"Look here!" he said, pointing to the ground.

I looked down. At my feet lay five or six silk handkerchiefs, torn and slashed and rent. I turned to him questioningly.

"They're what I tied the old woman up with," said he. "Fasten the horses and come along."

The handle of the door turned without resistance. We passed into the room which had been the scene of last night's bout. It was still strewn with the remnants of our meal and with empty bottles.

"Come in," cried Sapt, whose marvellous composure had at last almost given way.

We rushed down the passage towards the cellars. The door of the coal cellar stood wide open.

"They found the old woman," said I.

"You might have known that from the handkerchiefs," he said.

Then we came opposite the door of the wine cellar. It was shut. It looked in all respects as it had looked when we left it that morning.

"Come, it's all right," said I.

A loud oath from Sapt rang out. His face turned pale, and he pointed again at the floor. From under the door a red stain had spread over the floor of the passage and dried there. Sapt sank against the opposite wall. I tried the door. It was locked.

"Where's Josef?" muttered Sapt.

"Where's the king?" I responded.

Sapt took out a flask and put it to his lips. I ran back to the dining room and seized a heavy poker from the fireplace. In my terror and excitement I rained blows on the lock of the door, and I fired a cartridge into it. It gave way, and the door swung open.

"Give me a light," said I, but Sapt still leaned against the wall.

He was, of course, more moved than I, for he loved his master. Afraid for himself he was not—no man ever saw him that; but to think what might lie in that dark cellar was enough to turn any man's face pale. I went myself, and took a silver candlestick from the dining table and struck a light, and as I returned I felt the hot wax drip on my naked hand as the candle swayed to and fro, so that I cannot afford to despise Colonel Sapt for his agitation.

I came to the door of the cellar. The red stain, turning more and more to a dull brown, stretched inside. I walked two yards into the cellar and held the candle high above my head. I saw the full bins of wine; I saw spiders crawling on the walls; I saw, too, a couple of empty bottles lying on the floor; and then, away in the corner, I saw the body of a man, lying flat on his back, with his arms stretched wide and a crimson gash across his throat. I walked to him and knelt down beside him, and commended to God the soul of a faithful man. For it was the body of Josef, the little servant, slain in guarding the king.

I felt a hand on my shoulder, and, turning, saw Sapt's eyes, glaring and terror-struck, beside me.

"The king! My God! The king!" he whispered hoarsely.

I threw the candle's gleam over every inch of the cellar.

"The king is not here," said I.

7

His Majesty sleeps in Strelsau

I put my arm round Sapt's waist and supported him out of the cellar, drawing the battered door close after me. For ten minutes or more we sat silent in the dining room. Then old Sapt rubbed his knuckles into his eyes, gave one great gasp, and was himself again. As the clock on the mantelpiece struck one, he stamped his foot on the floor, saying, "They've got the king!"

"Yes," said I. "'All's well!' as Black Michael's dispatch said. What a moment it must have been for him when the royal salutes were fired at Strelsau this morning! I wonder when he got the message?"

"It must have been sent in the morning," said Sapt. "They must have sent it before news of your arrival at Strelsau reached Zenda—I suppose it came from Zenda."

"And he's carried it about all day!" I exclaimed. "Upon my honour, I'm not the only man who's had a trying day! What did he think, Sapt?"

"What does that matter? What does he think, lad, now?"

I rose to my feet.

"We must get back," I said, "and rouse every soldier in Strelsau. We ought to be in pursuit of Michael before midday."

Old Sapt pulled out his pipe and carefully lit it from the candle which guttered on the table.

"The king may be murdered while we sit here!" I urged.

Sapt smoked on for a moment in silence.

"That cursed old woman!" he broke out. "She must have attracted their attention somehow. I see the game. They came up to kidnap the king, and—as I say—somehow they found him. If you hadn't gone to Strelsau, you and I and Fritz had been in heaven by now!"

"And the king?"

"Who knows where the king is now?" he asked.

"Come, let's be off!" said I, but he sat still. And suddenly he burst into one of his grating chuckles: "By Jove, we've shaken up Black Michael!"

"Come, come!" I repeated impatiently.

"And we'll shake him up a bit more," he added, a cunning smile broadening on his wrinkled, weather-beaten face and his teeth working on an end of his grizzled moustache. "Aye, lad, we'll go back to Strelsau. The king shall be in his capital again tomorrow."

"The king?"

"The crowned king!"

"You're mad!" I cried.

"If we go back and tell the trick we played what would you give for our lives?"

"Just what they're worth," said I.

"And for the king's throne? Do you think that the nobles and the people will enjoy being fooled as you've fooled them? Do you think they'll love a king who was too drunk to be crowned and sent a servant to personate him?"

"He was drugged—and I'm no servant."

"Mine will be Black Michael's version."

He rose, came to me, and laid his hand on my shoulder.

"Lad," he said, "if you play the man you may save the king yet. Go back and keep his throne warm for him."

"But the duke knows—the villains he has employed know—"

"Aye, but they can't speak!" roared Sapt in grim triumph. "We've got 'em! How can they denounce you without denouncing themselves? 'This is not the king, because we kidnapped the king and murdered his servant.' Can they say that?"

The position flashed on me. Whether Michael knew me or not he could not speak. Unless he produced the king, what could he do? And if he produced the king where was he? For a moment I was carried away headlong, but in an instant the difficulties came strong upon me.

"I must be found out," I urged.

"Perhaps, but every hour's something. Above all, we must have a king in Strelsau, or the city will be Michael's in four-and-twenty hours, and what would the king's life be worth then—or his throne? Lad, you must do it!"

"Suppose they kill the king?"

"They'll kill him, if you don't."

"Sapt, suppose they have killed the king?"

"Then, my Heaven, you're as good an Elphberg as Black Michael, and you shall reign in Ruritania! But I don't believe they have; nor will they kill him if you're on the throne. Will they kill him to put you in?"

It was a wild plan—wilder even and more hopeless than the trick we had already carried through—but as I listened to Sapt I saw the strong points in our game. And then I was a young man and I loved action, and I was offered such a hand in such a game as perhaps never man played yet.

"I shall be found out," I said.

"Perhaps," said Sapt. "Come! To Strelsau! We shall be caught like rats in a trap if we stay here."

"Sapt," I cried. "I'll try it!"

"Well played!" said he. "I hope they've left us the horses. I'll go and see."

"We must bury that poor fellow," said I.

"No time," said Sapt.

"I'll do it."

"Hang you!" he grinned. "I make you a king, and—Well, do it. Go and fetch him, while I look to the horses. He can't lie very deep, but I doubt if he'll care about that. Poor little Josef! He was an honest bit of a man."

He went out, and I went to the cellar. I raised poor Josef in my arms and bore him into the passage and thence towards the door of the house. Just inside I laid him down, remembering that I must find spades for our task. At this instant Sapt came up.

"The horses are all right. There's the own brother to the one that brought you here. But you may save yourself that job."

"I'll not go before he's buried."

"Yes, you will."

"Not I, Colonel Sapt. Not for all Ruritania."

"You fool!" said he. "Come here."

He drew me to the door. The moon was sinking, but about three hundred yards away, coming along the road from Zenda, I made out a party of men. There were seven or eight of them; four were on horseback and the rest were walking, and I saw that they carried long implements, which I guessed to be spades and mattocks, on their shoulders.

"They'll save you the trouble," said Sapt. "Come along."

He was right. The approaching party must, beyond doubt, be Duke Michael's men, come to remove the traces of their evil work. I hesitated no longer, but an irresistible desire seized me. Pointing to the corpse of poor little Josef, I said to Sapt: "Colonel, we ought to strike a blow for him!"

"You'd like to give him some company, eh? But it's too risky work, your Majesty."

"I must have a slap at 'em," said I.

Sapt wavered. "Well," said he, "it's not business, you know; but you've been a good boy—and if we come to grief, why, hang me, it'll save us a lot of thinking! I'll show you how to touch them."

He cautiously closed the open chink of the door. Then we retreated through the house and made our way to the back entrance. Here our horses were standing. A carriage drive swept all round the lodge.

"Revolver ready?" asked Sapt.

"No; steel for me," said I.

"Gad, you're thirsty tonight," chuckled Sapt. "So be it."

We mounted, drawing our swords, and waited silently for a minute or two. Then we heard the tramp of men on the drive the other side of the house. They came to a stand, and one cried: "Now, then, fetch him out!"

"Now!" whispered Sapt.

Driving the spurs into our horses, we rushed at a gallop round the house, and in a moment we were among the ruffians. Sapt told me afterwards that he killed a man, and I believe him, but I saw no more of him. With a cut I split the head of a fellow on a brown horse, and he fell to the ground. Then I found myself opposite a big man, and I was half conscious of another to my right. It was too warm to stay, and with a simultaneous action I drove my spurs into my horse again and my sword full into the big man's breast. His bullet whizzed past my ear—I could almost swear it touched it. I wrenched at the sword, but it would not come, and I dropped it and galloped after Sapt, whom I now saw about twenty yards ahead. I waved my hand in farewell and dropped it a second later with a yell, for a bullet had grazed my finger and I felt the blood. Old Sapt turned round in the saddle. Someone fired again, but they had no rifles, and we were out of range. Sapt fell to laughing.

"That's one to me and two to you, with decent luck," said he. "Little Josef will have company."

"Aye, they'll be a *partie carrée*," said I. My blood was up, and I rejoiced to have killed them.

"Well, a pleasant night's work to the rest!" said he. "I wonder if they noticed you?"

"The big fellow did. As I struck him I heard him cry, 'The king!'"

"Good! Good! Oh, we'll give Black Michael some work before we've done!"

Pausing an instant, we made a bandage for my wounded finger, which was bleeding freely and ached severely, the bone being much bruised. Then we rode on, asking of our good horses all that was in them. The excitement of the fight and of our great resolve died away, and we rode in gloomy silence. Day broke clear and cold. We found a farmer just up, and made him give us sustenance for ourselves and our horses. I, feigning a toothache, muffled my face closely. Then ahead again till Strelsau lay before us. It was eight o'clock or nearing nine, and the gates were all open, as they always were save when the duke's caprice or intrigues shut them. We rode in by the same way as we had come out the evening before, all four of us—the men and the horses—wearied and jaded.

The streets were even quieter than when we had gone. Everyone was sleeping off last night's revelry, and we met hardly a soul till we reached the little gate of the palace. There Sapt's old groom was waiting for us.

"Is all well, sir?" he asked.

"All's well," said Sapt, and the man, coming to see, took my hand to kiss.

"The king's hurt!" he cried.

"It's nothing," said I as I dismounted. "I caught my finger in the door."

"Remember—silence!" said Sapt. "Ah! But, my good Freyler, I do not need to tell you that!"

The old fellow shrugged his shoulders.

"All young men like to ride abroad now and again. Why not the king?" said he, and Sapt's laugh left his opinion of my motives undisturbed.

"You should always trust a man," observed Sapt, fitting the key in the lock—"just as far as you must."

We went in and reached the dressing room. Flinging open the door, we saw Fritz von Tarlenheim stretched, fully dressed, on the sofa. He seemed to have been sleeping, but our entry woke him. He leaped to his feet, gave one glance at me, and with a joyful cry threw himself on his knees before me.

"Thank God, sire! Thank God, you're safe!" he cried, stretching his hand up to catch hold of mine.

I confess that I was moved. This king, whatever his faults, made people love him. For a moment I could not bear to speak or break the poor fellow's illusion. But tough old Sapt had no such feeling. He slapped his hand on his thigh delightedly.

"Bravo, lad!" cried he. "We shall do!"

Fritz looked up in bewilderment. I held out my hand.

"You're wounded, sire!" he exclaimed.

"It's only a scratch," said I, "but—" I paused.

He rose to his feet with a bewildered air. Holding my hand, he looked me up and down, and down and up. Then suddenly he dropped my hand and reeled back.

"Where's the king? Where's the king?" he cried.

"Hush, you fool!" hissed Sapt. "Not so loud! Here's the king!"
A knock sounded at the door. Sapt seized me by the hand.

"Here, quick, to the bedroom! Off with your cap and your boots. Get into bed. Cover everything up."

I did as I was bid. A moment later Sapt looked in, nodded, grinned, and introduced an extremely smart and deferential young gentleman, who came up to my bedside, bowing again and again, and informed me that he was of the household of the Princess Flavia and that her Royal Highness had sent him especially to inquire how the king's health was after the fatigues which his Majesty had undergone yesterday.

"My best thanks, sir, to my cousin," said I, "and tell her Royal Highness that I was never better in my life."

"The king," added old Sapt (who, I began to find, loved a good lie for its own sake), "has slept without a break all night."

The young gentleman (he reminded me of Osric in *Hamlet*) bowed himself out again. The farce was over, and Fritz von Tarlenheim's pale face recalled us to reality—though, in faith, the farce had to be reality for us now.

"Is the king dead?" he whispered.

"Please God, no," said I. "But he's in the hands of Black Michael!"

8

A Fair Cousin and a Dark Brother

A real king's life is perhaps a hard one, but a pretended king's is, I warrant, much harder. On the next day Sapt instructed me in my duties—what I ought to do and what I ought to know—for three hours, then I snatched breakfast, with Sapt still opposite me, telling me that the king always took white wine in the morning and was known to detest all highly seasoned dishes. Then came the chancellor for another three hours, and to him I had to explain that the hurt to my finger (we turned that bullet to happy account) prevented me from writing—whence arose great to-do, hunting of precedents and so forth, ending in my "making my mark", and the chancellor attesting it with a superfluity of solemn oaths. Then the French ambassador was introduced, to present his credentials; here my ignorance was of no importance, as the king would have been equally raw to the business (we worked through the whole *corps diplomatique* in the next few days, a demise of the crown necessitating all this bother).

Then, at last, I was left alone. I called my new servant (we had chosen, to succeed poor Josef, a young man who had never known the king), had a brandy and soda brought to me, and observed to Sapt that I trusted that I might now have a rest.

Fritz von Tarlenheim was standing by.

"By Heaven!" he cried, "we waste time. Aren't we going to throw Black Michael by the heels?"

"Gently, my son, gently," said Sapt, knitting his brows. "It would be a pleasure, but it might cost us dear. Would Michael fall and leave the king alive?"

"And," I suggested, "while the king is here in Strelsau, on his throne, what grievance has he against his dear brother Michael?"

"Are we to do nothing, then?"

"We're to do nothing stupid," growled Sapt.

"In fact, Fritz," said I, "I am reminded of a situation in one of our English plays—*The Critic*—have you heard of it? Or, if you like, of two men, each covering the other with a revolver. For I can't expose Michael without exposing myself—"

"And the king," put in Sapt.

"And, hang me, if Michael won't expose himself if he tries to expose me!"

"It's very pretty," said old Sapt.

"If I'm found out," I pursued, "I will make a clean breast of it and fight it out with the duke, but at present I'm waiting for a move from him."

"He'll kill the king," said Fritz.

"Not he," said Sapt.

"Half of the Six are in Strelsau," said Fritz.

"Only half? You're sure?" asked Sapt eagerly.

"Yes—only half."

"Then the king's alive, for the other three are guarding him!" cried Sapt.

"Yes—you're right!" exclaimed Fritz, his face brightening. "If the king were dead and buried they'd all be here with Michael. You know Michael's back, colonel?"

"I know, curse him!"

"Gentlemen, gentlemen," said I, "who are the Six?"

"I think you'll make their acquaintance soon," said Sapt. "They are six gentlemen whom Michael maintains in his household; they belong to him body and soul. There are three Ruritanians; then there's a Frenchman, a Belgian, and one of your countrymen."

"They'd all cut a throat if Michael told them," said Fritz.

"Perhaps they'll cut mine," I suggested.

"Nothing more likely," agreed Sapt. "Who are here, Fritz?"

"De Gautet, Bersonin, and Detchard."

"The foreigners! It's as plain as a pikestaff. He's brought them and left the Ruritanians with the king: that's because he wants to commit the Ruritanians as deep as he can."

"They were none of them among our friends at the lodge, then?" I asked.

"I wish they had been," said Sapt wistfully. "They had been not Six but Four by now."

I had already developed one attribute of royalty—a feeling that I need not reveal all my mind of my secret designs even to my intimate friends. I had fully resolved on my course of action. I meant to make myself as popular as I could, and at the same time to show no disfavour to Michael. By these means I hoped to allay the hostility of his adherents and make it appear, if an open conflict came about, that he was ungrateful and not oppressed.

Yet an open conflict was not what I hoped for.

The king's interest demanded secrecy, and while secrecy lasted I had a fine game to play in Strelsau. Michael should not grow stronger for delay!

I ordered my horse, and, attended by Fritz von Tarlenheim, rode in the grand new avenue of the royal park, returning all the salutes which I received with punctilious politeness. Then I rode through a few of the streets, stopped and bought flowers off a pretty girl, paying her with a piece of gold; and then, having attracted the desired amount of attention (for I had a trail of half a thousand people after me), I rode to the residence of the Princess Flavia and asked if she would receive me. This step created much interest and was met with shouts of approval. The princess was very popular, and the chancellor himself had not scrupled to hint to me that the more I pressed my suit and the more rapidly I brought it to a prosperous conclusion, the stronger would I be in the affection of my subjects. The chancellor, of course, did not understand the difficulties which lay in the way of following his loyal and excellent advice. However, I thought I could do no harm by calling; and in his view Fritz supported me with a cordiality that surprised me, until he confessed that he also had his motives for liking to visit the princess' house, which motive was no other than a great desire to see the princess's lady in waiting and bosom friend, the Countess Helga von Strofzin.

Etiquette seconded Fritz's hopes. While I was ushered into the princess's room, he remained with the countess in the antechamber. In spite of the people and servants who were hanging about, I doubt not that they managed a tête-à-tête, but I had no leisure to think of them for I was playing the most delicate move in all my difficult game. I had to keep the princess devoted to me—and yet indifferent to me. I had to show affection for her—and not feel it. I had to make love for another, and that to a girl who—princess or no princess—was the most beautiful I had ever seen. Well, I braced myself to the task, made no easier by the charming embarrassment with which I was received. How I succeeded in carrying out my programme will appear hereafter.

"You are gaining golden laurels," she said. "You are like the prince in Shakespeare who was transformed by becoming king. But I'm forgetting you are king, sire."

"I ask you to speak nothing but what your heart tells you—and to call me nothing but my name."

She looked at me for a moment. "Then I'm glad and proud, Rudolf," said she. "Why, as I told you, your very face is changed."

I acknowledged the compliment, but I disliked the topic; so I said, "My brother is back, I hear. He made an excursion, didn't he?"

"Yes, he is here," she said, frowning a little.

"He can't stay long from Strelsau, it seems," I observed, smiling. "Well, we are all glad to see him. The nearer he is the better."

The princess glanced at me with a gleam of amusement in her eyes.

"Why, cousin? Is it that you can—"

"See better what he's doing? Perhaps," said I. "And why are you glad?"

"I didn't say I was glad," she answered.

"Some people say so for you."

"There are many insolent people," she said, with delightful haughtiness.

"Possibly you mean that I am one?"

"Your Majesty could not be," she said, curtseying in feigned deference but adding, mischievously, after a pause, "Unless, that is—"

"Well, unless what?"

"Unless you tell me that I mind a snap of my fingers where the Duke of Strelsau is."

Really I wished that I had been the king.

"You don't care where Cousin Michael—"

"Ah, Cousin Michael! I call him the Duke of Strelsau."

"You call him Michael when you meet him?"

"Yes—by the orders of your father."

"I see. And now by mine?"

"If those are your orders."

"Oh, decidedly! We must all be pleasant to our dear Michael."

"You order me to receive his friends, too, I suppose?"

"The Six?"

"You call them that, too?"

"To be in the fashion I do. But I order you to receive no one unless you like."

"Except yourself?"

"I pray for myself. I could not order."

As I spoke there came a cheer from the street. The princess ran to the window.

"It is he!" she cried. "It is—the Duke of Strelsau!"

I smiled but said nothing. She returned to her seat. For a few moments we sat in silence. The noise outside subsided, but I heard the tread of feet in the anteroom. I began to talk on general subjects. This went on for some minutes. I wondered what had become of Michael, but it did not seem to be for me to interfere. All at once, to my great surprise, Flavia, clasping her hands, asked in an agitated voice:

"Are you wise to make him angry?"

"What? Who? How am I making him angry?"

"Why, by keeping him waiting."

"My dear cousin, I don't want to keep him—"

"Well, then, is he to come in?"

"Of course, if you wish it."

She looked at me curiously.

"How funny you are," she said. "Of course no one could be answered while I was with you."

Here was a charming attribute to royalty!

"An excellent etiquette!" I cried. "But I had clean forgotten it, and if I were alone with someone else couldn't you be announced?"

"You know as well as I do. I could be, because I am of the Blood," and she still looked puzzled.

"I never could remember all these silly rules," said I rather feebly as I inwardly cursed Fritz for not posting me up. "But I'll repair my fault."

I jumped up, flung open the door, and advanced into the anteroom. Michael was sitting at a table, a heavy frown on his face. Everyone else was standing, save that impudent young dog Fritz, who was lounging easily in an armchair and flirting with the Countess Helga. He leaped up as I entered, with a deferential elasticity that lent point to his former nonchalance. I had no difficulty in understanding that the duke might not like young Fritz.

I held out my hand. Michael took it, and I embraced him. Then I drew him with me into the inner room.

"Brother," I said, "if I had known you were here you should not have waited here a moment before I asked the princess to permit me to bring you to her."

He thanked me, but coldly. The man had many qualities, but he could not hide his feelings. A mere stranger could have seen that he hated me, and hated worse to see me with Princess Flavia, yet I am persuaded that he tried to conceal both feelings and, further, that he tried to persuade me that he believed I was verily the king. I did not know, of course, but unless the king were an impostor, at once cleverer and more audacious than I (and I began to think something of myself in that role), Michael could not believe that. And if he didn't how he must have loathed paying me deference and hearing my "Michael" and my "Flavia"!

"Your hand is hurt, sire," he observed with concern.

"Yes. I was playing a game with a mongrel dog (I meant to stir him), and you know, brother, such have uncertain tempers."

He smiled sourly, and his dark eyes rested on me for a moment.

"But is there no danger from the bite?" cried Flavia anxiously.

"None from this," said I. "If I gave him a chance to bite deeper it would be different, cousin."

"But surely he has been destroyed?" said she.

"Not yet. We're waiting to see if his bite is harmful."

"And if it is?" asked Michael with his sour smile.

"He'll be knocked on the head, brother," said I.

"You won't play with him any more?" urged Flavia.

"Perhaps I shall."

"He might bite again."

"Doubtless he'll try," said I, smiling.

Then, fearing Michael would say something which I must appear to resent (for, though I might show him my hate, I must seem to be full of favour), I began to compliment him on the magnificent condition of his regiment and on their loyal greeting to me on the day of my coronation. Thence I passed to a rapturous description of the shooting lodge which he had lent me. But he rose suddenly to his feet. His temper was failing him, and as an excuse he said farewell. However, as he reached the door he stopped, saying, "Three friends of mine are very anxious to have the honour of being presented to you, sire. They are here in the antechamber."

I joined him directly, passing my arm through his. The look on his face was honey to me. We entered the antechamber in fraternal fashion. Michael beckoned, and three men came forwards.

"These gentlemen," said Michael, with a stately courtesy which, to do him justice, he could assume with perfect grace and ease, "are the loyalest and most devoted of your Majesty's servants, and are my very faithful and attached friends."

"On the last ground as much as the first," said I, "I am very pleased to see them."

They came one by one and kissed my hand—De Gautet, a tall, lean fellow, with hair standing straight up and waxed moustache; Bersonin, the Belgian, a portly man of middle height with a bald head (though he was not far past thirty); and last, the Englishman, Detchard, a narrow-faced fellow with close-cut fair hair and a bronzed complexion. He was a finely made man, broad in the shoulders and slender in the hips. A good fighter but a crooked customer, I put him down for. I spoke to him in English with a slight foreign accent, and I swear the fellow smiled, though he hid the smile in an instant.

"So Mr Detchard is in the secret," thought I.

Having got rid of my dear brother and his friends, I returned to make my adieu to my cousin. She was standing at the door. I bade her farewell, taking her hand in mine.

"Rudolf," she said, very low, "be careful, won't you?"

"Of what?"

"You know—I can't say. But think what your life is to—"

"Well, to—?"

"To Ruritania."

Was I right to play the part, or wrong to play the part? I know not; evil lay both ways, and I dared not tell her the truth.

"Only to Ruritania?" I asked softly.

A sudden flush spread over her incomparable face.

"To your friends, too," she said.

"Friends?"

"And to your cousin," she whispered, "and loving servant."

I could not speak. I kissed her hand and went out cursing myself.

Outside I found Master Fritz, quite reckless of the footmen, playing at cat's-cradle with the Countess Helga.

"Hang it!" said he, "we can't always be plotting. Love claims his share."

"I'm inclined to think he does," said I, and Fritz, who had been by my side, dropped respectfully behind.

9

A New Use for a Tea Table

If I were to detail the ordinary events of my daily life at this time they might prove instructive to people who are not familiar with the insides of palaces; if I revealed some of the secrets I learned they might prove of interest to the statesmen of Europe. I intend to do neither of these things. I should be between the Scylla of dullness and the Charybdis of indiscretion, and I feel that I had far better confine myself strictly to the underground drama which was being played beneath the surface of Ruritanian politics. I need only say that the secret of my imposture defied detection. I made mistakes. I had bad minutes. It needed all the tact and graciousness whereof I was master to smooth over some apparent lapses of memory and unmindfulness of old acquaintances of which I was guilty. But I escaped, and I attributed my escape, as I have said before, most of all to the very audacity of the enterprise. It is my belief that, given the necessary physical likeness, it was far easier to pretend to be king of Ruritania than it would have been to personate my next-door neighbour.

One day Sapt came into my room. He threw me a letter, saying, "That's for you—a woman's hand, I think. But I've some news for you first."

"What's that?"

"The king's at the castle of Zenda," said he.

"How do you know?"

"Because the other half of Michael's Six are there. I had inquiries made, and they're all there—Lauengram, Krafstein, and young Rupert Hentzau; three rogues, too, on my honour, as fine as live in Ruritania."

"Well?"

"Well, Fritz wants you to march to the castle with horse, foot, and artillery."

"And drag the moat?" I asked.

"That would be about it," grinned Sapt, "and we shouldn't find the king's body then."

"You think it's certain he's there?"

"Very probable. Besides the fact of those three being there, the drawbridge is kept up and no one goes in without an order from young Hentzau or Black Michael himself. We must tie Fritz up."

"I'll go to Zenda," said I.

"You're mad."

"Some day."

"Oh, perhaps. You'll very likely stay there, though, if you do."

"That may be, my friend," said I carelessly.

"His Majesty looks sulky," observed Sapt. "How's the love affair?"

Damn you, hold your tongue!" I said.

He looked at me for a moment, then he lit his pipe. It was quite true that I was in a bad temper, and I went on perversely, "Wherever I go I'm dogged by half a dozen fellows."

"I know you are. I send 'em," he replied composedly.

"What for?"

"Well," said Sapt, puffing away, "it wouldn't be exactly inconvenient for Black Michael if you disappeared. With you gone the old game that we stopped would be played—or he'd have a shot at it."

"I can take care of myself."

"De Gautet, Bersonin, and Detchard are in Strelsau. and any one of them, lad, would cut your throat as readily—as readily as I would Black Michael's and a deal more treacherously. What's the letter?"

I opened it and read it aloud:

"If the king desires to know what it deeply concerns the king to know let him do as this letter bids him. At the end of the New Avenue there stands a house in large grounds. The house has a portico, with a statue of a nymph in it. A wall encloses the garden. There is a gate in the wall at the back. At twelve o'clock tonight, if the king enters alone by that gate, turns to the right, and walks twenty yards, he will find a summerhouse, approached by a flight of six steps. If he mounts and enters he will find someone who will tell him what touches most dearly his life and his throne. This is written by a faithful friend. He must be alone. If he neglects the invitation his life will be in danger. Let him show this to no one, or he will ruin a woman who loves him: Black Michael does not pardon."

"No," observed Sapt as I ended, "but he can dictate a very pretty letter."

I had arrived at the same conclusion and was about to throw the letter away when I saw there was more writing on the other side.

"Hallo! There's some more."

"If you hesitate" [the writer continued] "consult Colonel Sapt—"

"Eh!" exclaimed that gentleman, genuinely astonished. "Does she take me for a greater fool than you?"

I waved to him to be silent.

"Ask him what woman would do most to prevent the duke from marry ing his cousin, and therefore most to prevent his becoming king? And ask if her name begins with—A."

I sprang to my feet. Sapt laid down his pipe.

"Antoinette de Mauban, by Heaven!" I cried.

"How do you know?" asked Sept.

I told him what I knew of the lady and how I knew it. He nodded.

"It's so far true that she's had a great row with Michael" said he thoughtfully.

"If she would she could be useful," I said.

"I believe, though, that Michael wrote that letter."

"So do I, but I mean to know for certain. I shall go, Sapt."

"No, I shall go," said he.

"You may go as far as the gate."

"I shall go to the summerhouse."

"I'm hanged if you shall!"

I rose and leaned my back against the mantelpiece.

"Sapt, I believe in that woman, and I shall go."

"I don't believe in any woman," said Sapt, "and you shan't go."

"I either go to the summerhouse or back to England," said I.

Sapt began to know exactly how far he could lead or drive, and when he must follow.

"We're playing against time," I added. "Every day we leave the king where he is there is fresh risk. Every day I masquerade like this there is fresh risk. Sapt, we must play high. We must force the game."

"So be it," he said with a sigh.

To cut the story short, at half-past eleven that night Sapt and I mounted our horses. Fritz was again left on guard, our destination not being revealed to him. It was a very dark night. I wore no sword, but I carried a revolver, a long knife, and a bull's-eye lantern. We arrived outside the gate. I dismounted. Sapt held out his hand.

"I shall wait here," he said. "If I hear a shot I'll—"

"Stay where you are. It's the king's only chance. You mustn't come to grief too."

"You're right, lad. Good luck!"

I pressed the little gate. It yielded, and I found myself in a wild sort of shrubbery. There was a grass-grown path and, turning to the right as I had been bidden, I followed it cautiously. My lantern was closed, the revolver was in my hand. I heard not a sound. Presently a large dark object loomed out of the gloom ahead of me. It was the summerhouse. Reaching the steps, I mounted them and found myself confronted by a weak, rickety wooden door, which hung upon the latch. I pushed it open and walked in. A woman flew to me and seized my hand.

"Shut the door," she whispered.

I obeyed and turned the light of my lantern on her. She was in evening dress, arrayed very sumptuously, and her dark striking beauty was marvellously displayed in the glare of the bull's-eye. The summerhouse was a bare little room, furnished only with a couple of chairs and a small iron table, such as one sees in a tea garden or an open-air cafe.

"Don't talk," she said. "We've no time. Listen! I know you, Mr Rassendyll. I wrote that letter at the duke's orders."

"So I thought," said I.

"In twenty minutes three men will be here to kill you."

"Three—the three?"

"Yes. You must be gone by then. If not tonight you'll be killed—"

"Or they will."

"Listen, listen! When you're killed your body will be taken to a low quarter of the town. It will be found there. Michael will at once arrest all your friends—Colonel Sapt and Captain von Tarlenheim first—proclaim a state of siege in Strelsau, and send a messenger to Zenda. The other three will murder the king in the castle, and the duke will proclaim either himself or the princess—himself if he is strong enough. Anyhow, he'll marry her, and become king in fact and soon in name. Do you see?"

"It's a pretty plot. But why, madame, do you—"

"Say I'm a Christian—or say I'm jealous. My God! Shall I see him marry her? Now go, but remember—this is what I have to tell you—that never by night or by day are you safe. Three men follow you as a guard. Is it not so? Well, three follow them. Michael's three are never two hundred yards from you. Your life is not worth a moment if ever they find you alone. Now go. Stay, the gate will be guarded by now. Go down softly, go past the summerhouse, on for a hundred yards, and you'll find a ladder against the wall. Get over it and fly for your life."

"And you?" I asked.

"I have my game to play, too. If he finds out what I have done we shall not meet again. If not I may yet—But never mind. Go at once."

"But what will you tell him?"

"That you never came—that you saw through the trick."

I took her hand and kissed it.

"Madame," said I, "you have served the king well tonight. Where is he in the castle?"

She sank her voice to a fearful whisper. I listened eagerly.

"Across the drawbridge you come to a heavy door. Behind that lies—Hark! What's that?"

There were steps outside.

"They're coming! They're too soon! Heavens! They're too soon!" and she turned pale as death.

"They seem to me," said I, "to be in the nick of time."

"Close your lantern. See, there's a chink in the door. Can you see them?"

I put my eye to the chink. On the lowest step I saw three dim figures. I cocked my revolver. Antoinette hastily laid her hand on mine.

"You may kill one," said she. "But what then?"

A voice came from outside—a voice that spoke perfect English. "Mr Rassendyll," it said.

I made no answer.

"We want to talk to you. Will you promise not to shoot till we've done?"

"Have I the pleasure of addressing Mr Detchard?" I said.

"Never mind names."

"Then let mine alone."

"All right, sire. I've an offer for you."

I still had my eye to the chink. The three had mounted two steps more; three revolvers pointed full at the door.

"Will you let us in? We pledge our honour to observe the truce."

"Don't trust them," whispered Antoinette.

"We can speak through the door," said I.

"But you might open it and fire," objected Detchard, "and though we should finish you, you might finish one of us. Will you give your honour not to fire while we talk?"

"Don't trust them," whispered Antoinette again.

A sudden idea struck me. I considered it for a moment. It seemed feasible.

"I give my honour not to fire before you do," said I, "but I won't let you in. Stand outside and talk."

"That's sensible," he said.

The three mounted the last step and stood just outside the door. I laid my ear to the chink. I could hear no words, but Detchard's head was close to that of the taller of his companions (De Gautet, I guessed).

"H'm! Private communications," thought I. Then I said aloud, "Well, gentlemen, what's the offer?"

"A safe conduct to the frontier, and fifty thousand pounds English."

"No, no," whispered Antoinette in the lowest of whispers. "They are treacherous."

"That seems handsome," said I, reconnoitring through the chink. They were all close together, just outside the door now.

I had probed the hearts of the ruffians, and I did not need Antoinette's warning. They meant to "rush" me as soon as I was engaged in talk.

"Give me a minute to consider," said I, and I thought I heard a laugh outside.

I turned to Antoinette.

"Stand up close to the wall, out of the line of fire from the door," I whispered.

"What are you going to do?" she asked in fright.

"You'll see," said I.

I took up the little iron table. It was not very heavy for a man of my strength, and I held it by the legs. The top, protruding in front of me, made a complete screen for my head and body. I fastened my closed lantern to my belt and put my revolver in a handy pocket. Suddenly I saw the door move ever so slightly—perhaps it was the wind, perhaps it was a hand trying it outside.

I drew back as far as I could from the door, holding the table in the position that I have described. Then I called out: "Gentlemen, I accept your offer, relying on your honour. If you will open the door—"

"Open it yourself," said Detchard.

"It opens outwards," said I. "Stand back a little, gentlemen, or I shall hit you when I open it."

I went and fumbled with the latch. Then I stole back to my place on tiptoe.

"I can't open it!" I cried. "The latch has caught."

"Tut! I'll open it!" cried Detchard. "Nonsense, Bersonin, why not? Are you afraid of one man?"

I smiled to myself. An instant later the door was flung back.

The gleam of a lantern showed me the three close together outside, their revolvers levelled. With a shout I charged at my utmost pace across the summerhouse and through the doorway. Three shots rang out and battered into my shield. Another moment, and I leaped out and the table caught them full and square, and in a tumbling, swearing, struggling mass they and I and that brave table rolled down the steps of the summerhouse to the ground below. Antoinette de Mauban shrieked, but I rose to my feet, laughing aloud.

De Gautet and Bersonin lay like men stunned. Detchard was under the table, but as I rose he pushed it from him and fired again. I raised my revolver and took a snap shot. I heard him curse, and then I ran like a hare, laughing as I went, past the summerhouse and along by the wall. I heard steps behind me, and, turning round, I fired again for luck. The steps ceased.

"Please God," said I, "she told me the truth about the ladder!" for the wall was high and topped with iron spikes.

Yes, there it was. I was up and over in a minute. Doubling back, I saw the horses. Then I heard a shot. It was Sapt. He had heard us and was battling and raging with the locked gate, hammering it and firing into the keyhole like a man possessed. He had quite forgotten that he was not to take part in the fight. Whereat I laughed again and said as I clapped him on the shoulder, "Come home to bed, old chap. I've got the finest tea-table story that ever you heard!"

He started and cried: "You're safe!" and wrung my hand. But a moment later he added:

"And what the devil are you laughing at?"

"Four gentlemen round a tea table," said I, laughing still, for it had been uncommonly ludicrous to see the formidable three altogether routed and scattered with no more deadly weapon than an ordinary tea table.

Moreover, you will observe that I had honourably kept my word and not fired till they did.

10

A Great Chance for a Villain

It was the custom that the prefect of police should send every afternoon a report to me on the condition of the capital and the feeling of the people. The document included also an account of the movements of any persons whom the police had received instructions to watch. Since I had been in Strelsau, Sapt had been in the habit of reading the report and telling me any items of interest which it might contain. On the day after my adventure in the summerhouse he came in as I was playing a hand of écarte with Fritz von Tarlenheim.

"The report is rather full of interest this afternoon," he observed, sitting down.

"Do you find," I asked, "any mention of a certain fracas?"

He shook his head with a smile.

"I find this first," he said: "'His Highness the Duke of Strelsau left the city (so far as it appears, suddenly), accompanied by several of his household. His destination is believed to be the castle of Zenda, but the party travelled by road and not by train. MM. De Gautet, Bersonin, and Detchard followed an hour later, the last named carrying his arm in a sling. The cause of his wound is not known, but it is suspected that he has fought a duel, probably incidental to a love affair.'"

"That is remotely true," I observed, very well pleased to find that I had left my mark on the fellow.

"Then we come to this," pursued Sapt, "'Mme de Mauban, whose movements have been watched according to instructions, left by train at midday. She took a ticket for Dresden—'"

"It's an old habit of hers," said I.

"'The Dresden trains stop at Zenda.' An acute fellow, this. And finally listen to this: 'The state of feeling in the city is not satisfactory. The king is much criticized' (you know he's told to be quite frank) 'for taking no steps about his marriage.' From inquiries among the entourage of the Princess Flavia, her Royal Highness is believed to be deeply offended by the remissness of his Majesty. The common people are coupling her name with that of the Duke of Strelsau, and the duke gains much popularity from the suggestion. I have caused the announcement that the king gives a ball tonight in honour of the princess to be widely diffused, and the effect is good."

"That is news to me," said I.

"Oh, the preparations are all made!" laughed Fritz. "I've seen to that."

Sapt turned to me and said in a sharp, decisive voice, "You must make love to her tonight, you know."

"I think it very likely I shall if I see her alone," said I. "Hang it, Sapt, you don't suppose I find it difficult?"

Fritz whistled a bar or two, then he said, "You'll find it only too easy. Look here, I hate telling you this, but I must. The Countess Helga told me that the princess had become most attached to the king. Since the coronation her feelings have undergone a marked development. It's quite true that she is deeply wounded by the king's apparent neglect."

"Here's a kettle of fish!" I groaned.

"Tut, tut!" said Sapt. "I suppose you've made pretty speeches to a girl before now? That's all she wants."

Fritz, himself a lover, understood better my distress. He laid his hand on my shoulder, but said nothing.

"I think, though," pursued that cold-blooded old Sapt, "that you'd better make your offer tonight."

"Good Heavens!"

"Or, at any rate, go near it, and I shall send a 'semi-official' to the papers."

"I'll do nothing of the sort—no more will you!" said I. "I utterly refuse to take part in making a fool of the princess."

Sapt looked at me with his small keen eyes. A slow, cunning smile passed over his face.

"All right, lad, all right," said he. "We mustn't press you too hard. Soothe her down a bit, if you can, you know. Now for Michael!"

"Oh, damn Michael!" said I. "He'll do tomorrow. Here, Fritz, come for a stroll in the garden."

Sapt at once yielded. His rough manner covered a wonderful tact—and, as I came to recognize more and more, a remarkable knowledge of human nature. Why did he urge me so little about the princess? Because he knew that her beauty and my ardour would carry me further than all his arguments—and that the less I thought about the thing the more likely was I to do it. He must have seen the unhappiness he might bring on the princess, but that went for nothing with him. Can I say, confidently, that he was wrong? If the king were restored the princess must turn to him, either knowing or not knowing the change. And if the king were not restored to us? It was a subject that we had never yet spoken of. But I had an idea that, in such a case, Sapt meant to seat me on the throne of Ruritania for the term of my life. He would have set Satan himself there sooner than that pupil of his, Black Michael.

The ball was a sumptuous affair. I opened it by dancing a quadrille with Flavia, then I waltzed with her. Curious eyes and eager whispers attended us. We went in to supper, and halfway through I, half mad by then, for her glance had answered mine, and her quick breathing met my stammered sentences—I rose in my place before all the brilliant crowd, and taking the Red Rose that I wore, flung the ribbon with its jewelled badge round her neck. In a tumult of applause I sat down. I saw Sapt smiling over his wine, and Fritz frowning. The rest of the meal passed in silence; neither Flavia nor I could speak. Fritz touched me on the shoulder, and I rose, gave her my arm, and walked down the hall into a little room, where coffee was served to us. The gentlemen and ladies in attendance withdrew, and we were alone.

The little room had French windows opening on the gardens. The night was fine, cool and fragrant. Flavia sat down, and I stood opposite her. I was struggling with myself; if she had not looked at me I believe that even then I should have won my fight. But suddenly, involuntarily, she gave me one brief glance—a glance of question, hurriedly turned aside; a blush that the question had overcome spread over her cheek, and she caught her breath.

Ah, if you had seen her! I forgot the king in Zenda. I forgot the king in Strelsau. She was a princess—and I an impostor. Do you think I remembered that? I threw myself on my knee and seized her hands in mine. I said nothing. Why should I? The soft sounds of the night set my wooing to a wordless melody as I pressed my kisses on her lips.

She pushed me from her, crying suddenly: "Ah! Is it true? Or is it only because you must?"

"It's true!" I said in low, smothered tones—"true that I love you more than life—or truth—or honour!"

She set no meaning to my words, treating them as one of love's sweet extravagances. She came close to me and whispered: "Oh, if you were not the king! Then I could show you how I love you! How is it that I love you now, Rudolf?"

"Now?"

"Yes—just lately. I—I never did before."

Pure triumph filled me. It was I—Rudolf Rassendyll—who had won her! I caught her round the waist.

"You didn't love me before?" I asked.

She looked up into my face, smiling, as she whispered, "It must have been your crown. I felt it first on the coronation day."

"Never before?" I asked eagerly.

She laughed low.

"You speak as if you would be pleased to hear me say 'Yes' to that," she said.

"Would 'Yes' be true?"

"Yes," I just heard her breathe, and she went on in an instant: "Be careful, Rudolf. Be careful, dear. He will be mad now."

"What, Michael? If Michael were the worst—"

"What worst is there?"

There was yet a chance for me. Controlling myself with a mighty effort, I took my hands off her and stood a yard or two away. I remember now the note of the wind in the elm trees outside.

"If I were not the king," I began, "if I were only a private gentleman—"

Before I could finish her hand was in mine.

"If you were a convict in the prison of Strelsau you would be my king," she said.

And under my breath I groaned, "God forgive me!" and, holding her hand in mine, I said again, "If I were not the king—"

"Hush, hush!" she whispered. "I don't deserve it—I don't deserve to be doubted. Ah, Rudolf! Does a woman who marries without love look on the man as I look on you?"

And she hid her face from me.

For more than a minute we stood there together, and I, even with my arm about her, summoned up what honour and conscience her beauty and the toils that I was in had left me.

"Flavia," I said in a strange, dry voice that seemed not my own, "I am not—"

As I spoke—as she raised her eyes to me—there was a heavy step on the gravel outside, and a man appeared at the window. A little cry burst from Flavia as she sprang back from me. My half-finished sentence died on my lips. Sapt stood there, bowing low but with a stern frown on his face.

"A thousand pardons, sire," said he, "but his Eminence the Cardinal has waited this quarter of an hour to offer his respectful adieu to your Majesty."

I met his eye full and square, and I read in it an angry warning. How long he had been a listener I knew not, but he had come in upon us in the nick of time.

"We must not keep his Eminence waiting," said I.

But Flavia, in whose love there lay no shame, with radiant eyes and blushing face held out her hand to Sapt. She said nothing, but no man could have missed her meaning who had ever seen a woman in the exaltation of love. A sour, yet sad, smile passed over the old soldier's face, and there was tenderness in his voice as, bending to kiss her hand, he said, "In joy and sorrow, in good times and bad. God save your Royal Highness!"

He paused and added, glancing at me and drawing himself up to military erectness, "But before all comes the king—God save the king!"

And Flavia caught at my hand and kissed it, murmuring, "Amen! Good God, amen!"

We went into the ballroom again. Forced to receive adieus, I was separated from Flavia; everyone, when he left me, went to her. Sapt was out and in of the throng, and where he had been glances, smiles, and whispers were rife. I doubted not that, true to his relentless purpose, he was spreading the news that he had learned. To uphold the crown and beat Black Michael—that was his one resolve. Flavia, myself—aye, and the real king in Zenda, were pieces in his game, and pawns have no business with passions. Not even at the walls of the palace did he stop; for when at last I handed Flavia down the broad marble steps and into her carriage there was a great crowd awaiting us, and we were welcomed with deafening cheers. What could I do? Had I spoken then they would have refused to believe that I was not the king; they might have believed that the king had run mad. By Sapt's devices and my own ungoverned passion I had been forced on, and the way back had closed behind me; and the passion still drove me in the same direction as the devices seduced me. I faced all Strelsau that night as the king and the accepted suitor of the Princess Flavia.

At last, at three in the morning, when the cold light of dawning day began to steal in, I was in my dressing room, and Sapt alone was with me. I sat like a man dazed, staring into the fire; he puffed at his pipe; Fritz was gone to bed, having almost refused to speak to me. On the table by me lay a rose; it had been in Flavia's dress, and as we parted she had kissed it and given it to me.

Sapt advanced his hand towards the rose, but, with a quick movement, I shut mine down upon it.

"That's mine," I said, "not yours—nor the king's either."

"We struck a good blow for the king tonight," said he.

I turned on him fiercely.

"What's to prevent me striking a blow for myself?" I said.

He nodded his head.

"I know what's in your mind," he said. "Yes, lad, but you're bound in honour."

"Have you left me any honour?"

"Oh, come, to play a little trick on a girl—"

"You can spare me that. Colonel Sapt, if you would not have me utterly a villain—if you would not have your king rot in Zenda, while Michael and I play for the great stake outside—You follow me?"

"Aye, I follow you."

"We must act, and quickly! You saw tonight—you heard tonight—"

"I did," said he.

"Your cursed acuteness told you what I should do. Well, leave me here a week—and there's another problem for you. Do you find the answer?"

"Yes, I find it," he answered, frowning heavily. "But if you did that you'd have to fight me first—and kill me."

"Well, and if I had—or a score of men? I tell you, I could raise all Strelsau on you in an hour, and choke you with your lies—yes, your mad lies—in your mouth."

"It's gospel truth," he said—"thanks to my advice, you could."

"I could marry the princess, and send Michael and his brother together to—"

"I'm not denying it, lad," said he.

"Then, in God's name," I cried, stretching out my hands to him, "let us go to Zenda and crush this Michael and bring the king back to his own again."

The old fellow stood and looked at me for full a minute.

"And the princess?" he said.

I bowed my head to meet my hands and crushed the rose between my fingers and my lips.

I felt his hand on my shoulder, and his voice sounded husky as he whispered low in my ear, "Before God, you're the finest Elphberg of them all. But I have eaten of the king's bread, and I am the king's servant. Come, we will go to Zenda!"

And I looked up and caught him by the hand. And the eyes of both of us were wet.

11

Hunting a Very Big Boar

The terrible temptation which was assailing me will now be understood. I would so force Michael's hand that he must kill the king. I was in a position to bid him defiance and tighten my grasp on the crown—not for its own sake but because the King of Ruritania was to wed the Princess Flavia. What of Sapt and Fritz? Ah! But a man cannot be held to write down in cold blood the wild and black thoughts that storm his brain when an uncontrolled passion has battered a breach for them. Yet, unless he sets up as a saint, he need not hate himself for them. He is better employed, as it humbly seems to me, in giving thanks that power to resist was vouchsafed to him than in fretting over wicked impulses which come unsought and extort an unwilling hospitality from the weakness of our nature.

It was a fine bright morning when I walked, unattended, to the princess's house, carrying a nosegay in my hand. Policy made excuses for love, and every attention that I paid her, while it riveted my own chains, bound closer to me the people of the great city, who worshipped her. I found Fritz's inamorata, the Countess Helga, gathering blooms in the garden for her mistress's wear, and prevailed on her to take mine in their place. The girl was rosy with happiness, for Fritz, in his turn, had not wasted his evening, and no dark shadow hung over his wooing save the hatred which the Duke of Strelsau was known to bear him.

"And that," she said with a mischievous smile, "your Majesty has made of no moment. Yes, I will take the flowers. Shall I tell you, sire, what is the first thing the princess does with them?"

We were talking on a broad terrace that ran along the back of the house, and a window above our heads stood open.

"Madame!" cried the countess merrily, and Flavia herself looked out. I bared my head and bowed. She wore a white gown, and her hair was loosely gathered in a knot. She kissed her hand to me, crying, "Bring the king up, Helga. I'll give him some coffee."

The countess, with a bright glance, led the way and took me into Flavia's morning room. And, left alone, we greeted one another as lovers are wont. Then the princess laid two letters before me. One was from Black Michael—a most courteous request that she would honour him by spending a day at his castle of Zenda, as had been her custom once a year in the summer, when the place and its gardens were in the height of their great beauty. I threw the letter down in disgust, and Flavia laughed at me. Then, growing grave again, she pointed to the other sheet.

"I don't know who that comes from," she said. "Read it."

I knew in a moment. There was no signature at all this time, but the handwriting was the same as that which had told me of the snare in the summerhouse; it was Antoinette de Mauban's.

> I have no cause to love you [it ran], but God forbid that you should fall into the power of the duke. Accept no invitations of his. Go nowhere without a large guard—a regiment is not too much to make you safe. Show this if you can to him who reigns in Strelsau.

"Why doesn't it say 'the king'?" asked Flavia, leaning over my shoulder so that the ripple of her hair played on my cheek. "Is it a hoax?"

"As you value life, and more than life, my queen," I said, "obey it to the very letter. A regiment shall camp round your house to-day. See that you do not go out unless well guarded."

"An order, sire?" she asked, a little rebellious.

"Yes, an order, madame—if you love me."

"Ah!" she cried, and I could not but kiss her.

"You know who sent it?" she asked.

"I guess," said I. "It is from a good friend—and, I fear, an unhappy woman. You must be ill, Flavia, and unable to go to Zenda. Make your excuses as cold and formal as you like."

"So you feel strong enough to anger Michael?" she said with a proud smile.

"I'm strong enough for anything while you are safe," said I.

Soon I tore myself away from her, and then, without consulting Sapt, I took my way to the house of Marshal Strakencz. I had seen something of the old general, and I liked and trusted him. Sapt was less enthusiastic, but I had learned by now that Sapt was best pleased when he could do everything, and jealousy played some part in his views. As things were now, I had more work than Sapt and Fritz could manage, for they must come with me to Zenda, and I wanted a man to guard what I loved most in all the world, and suffer me to set about my task of releasing the king with a quiet mind.

The marshal received me with most loyal kindness. To some extent I took him into my confidence. I charged him with the care of the princess, looking him full and significantly in the face as I bade him let no one from her cousin the duke approach her unless he himself were there and a dozen of his men with him.

"You may be right, sire," said he, shaking his grey head sadly. "I have known better men than the duke do worse things than that for love."

I could quite appreciate the remark, but I said, "There's something besides love, marshal. Love's for the heart. Is there nothing my brother might like for his head?"

"I pray that you wrong him, sire."

"Marshal, I'm leaving Strelsau for a few days. Every evening I will send a courier to you. If for three days none comes, you will publish an order which I will give you, depriving Duke Michael of the governorship of Strelsau and appointing you in his place. You will declare a state of siege. Then you will send word to Michael that you demand an audience of the king—You follow me?"

"Aye, sire."

"In twenty-four hours, if he does not produce the king"—I laid

my hand on his knee—"then the king is dead, and you will proclaim the next heir. You know who that is?"

"The Princess Flavia."

"And swear to me, on your faith and honour, and by the fear of
the living God, that you will stand by her to your death, and kill
that reptile, and seat her where I sit now."

"On my faith and honour, and by the fear of God, I swear it!
And may Almighty God preserve your Majesty, for I think that
you go on an errand of danger."

"I hope that no life more precious than mine may be demanded," said I, rising. Then I held out my hand to him.

"Marshal," I said, "in days to come it may be—I know not—
that you will hear strange things of the man who speaks to you
now. Let him be what he may, and who he may, what say you of
the manner in which he has borne himself as king in Strelsau?"

The old man, holding my hand, spoke to me, man to man.

"I have known many of the Elphbergs," said he, "and I have
seen you. And, happen what may, you have borne yourself as a
wise king and a brave man; aye, and you have proved as courteous a gentleman and as gallant a lover as any that have been of the
House."

"Be that my epitaph," said I, "when the time comes that another
sits on the throne of Ruritania."

"God send a far day, and may I not see it!" said he.

I was much moved, and the marshal's worn face twitched. I sat
down and wrote my order.

"I can hardly yet write," said I. "My finger is stiff still."

It was, in fact, the first time I had ventured to write more than a
signature, and in spite of the pains I had taken to learn the king's
hand I was not yet perfect in it.

"Indeed, sire," he said, "it differs a little from your ordinary handwriting. It is unfortunate, for it may lead to suspicion of forgery."

"Marshal," said I with a laugh, "what use are the guns of
Strelsau if they can't assuage a little suspicion?"

He smiled grimly and took the paper.

"Colonel Sapt and Fritz von Tarlenheim go with me," I continued.

"You go to seek the duke?" he asked in a low tone.

"Yes, the duke, and someone else of whom I have need and who is at Zenda," I replied.

"I wish I could go with you," he cried, tugging at his white moustache. "I'd like to strike a blow for you and your crown."

"I leave you what is more than my life and more than my crown," said I, "because you are the man I trust more than all others in Ruritania."

"I will deliver her to you safe and sound," said he, "and, failing that, I will make her queen."

We parted, and I returned to the palace and told Sapt and Fritz what I had done. Sapt had a few faults to find and a few grumbles to utter. This was merely what I expected, for Sapt liked to be consulted beforehand, not informed afterwards. On the whole, he approved of my plans, and his spirits rose high as the hour of action drew nearer and nearer. Fritz, too, was ready; though he, poor fellow, risked more than Sapt did, for he was a lover, and his happiness hung in the scale. Yet how I envied him! For the triumphant issue which would crown him with happiness and unite him to his mistress, the success for which we were bound to hope and strive and struggle, meant to me sorrow more certain and greater than if I were doomed to fail. He understood something of this, for when we were alone (save for old Sapt, who was smoking at the other end of the room) he passed his arm through mine, saying, "It's hard for you. Don't think I don't trust you. I know you have nothing but true thoughts in your heart."

But I turned away from him, thankful that he could not see what my heart held but only be witness to the deeds that my hands were to do.

Yet even he did not understand, for he had not dared to lift his eyes to the Princess Flavia, as I had lifted mine.

Our plans were now all made, even as we proceeded to carry them out, and as they will hereafter appear. The next morning we were to start on the hunting excursion. I had made all arrangements for being absent, and now there was only one thing left to do—the hardest, the most heartbreaking. As evening fell I drove through the busy streets to Flavia's residence. I was recognized as

I went and heartily cheered. I played my part and made shift to look the happy lover. In spite of my depression I was almost amused at the coolness and delicate hauteur with which my sweet lover received me. She had heard that the king was leaving Strelsau on a hunting expedition.

"I regret that we cannot amuse your Majesty here in Strelsau," she said, tapping her foot lightly on the floor. "I would have offered you more entertainment, but I was foolish enough to think—"

"Well, what?" I asked, leaning over her.

"That for just a day or two, after—after last night—you might be happy without much gaiety," and she turned pettishly from me as she added, "I hope the boars will be more engrossing."

"I'm going after a very big boar," said I, and, because I could not help it, I began to play with her hair, but she moved her head away.

"Are you offended with me?" I asked in feigned surprise, for I could not resist tormenting her a little. I had never seen her angry, and every fresh aspect of her was a delight to me.

"What right have I to be offended? True, you said last night that every hour away from me was wasted. But a very big boar! That's a different thing."

"Perhaps the boar will hunt me," I suggested. "Perhaps, Flavia, he'll catch me."

She made no answer.

"You are not touched even by that danger?"

Still she said nothing, and I, stealing round, found her eyes full of tears.

"You weep for my danger?"

Then she spoke very low, "This is like what you used to be, but not like the king—the king I—I have come to love!"

With a sudden great groan I caught her to my heart.

"My darling!" I cried, forgetting everything but her, "did you dream that I left you to go hunting?"

"What then, Rudolf? Ah! You're not going—"

"Well, it is hunting. I go to seek Michael in his lair."

She had turned very pale.

"So you see, sweet, I was not so poor a lover as you thought me. I shall not be long gone."

"You will write to me, Rudolf?"

I was weak, but I could not say a word to stir suspicion in her.

"I'll send you all my heart every day," said I.

"And you'll run no danger?"

"None that I need not."

"And when will you be back? Ah, how long it will be!"

"When shall I be back?" I repeated.

"Yes, yes! Don't be long, dear, don't be long. I shan't sleep while you're away."

"I don't know when I shall be back," said I.

"Soon, Rudolf, soon?"

"God knows, my darling. But if never—"

"Hush, hush!" and she pressed her lips to mine.

"If never," I whispered, "you must take my place. You'll be the only one of the House then. You must reign and not weep for me."

For a moment she drew herself up like a very queen.

"Yes, I will!" she said. "I will reign. I will do my part, though all my life will be empty and my heart dead, yet I'll do it!"

She paused, and sinking against me again, wailed softly, "Come soon! Come soon!"

Carried away, I cried loudly, "As God lives, I—yes, I myself—will see you once more before I die!"

"What do you mean?" she exclaimed with wondering eyes, but I had no answer for her, and she gazed at me with her wondering eyes.

I dared not ask her to forget; she would have found it an insult. I could not tell her then who and what I was. She was weeping and I had but to dry her tears.

"Shall a man not come back to the loveliest lady in all the wide world?" said I. "A thousand Michaels should not keep me from you!"

She clung to me, a little comforted.

"You won't let Michael hurt you?"

"No, sweetheart."

"Or keep you from me?"

"No, sweetheart."

"Nor anyone else?"

And again I answered, "No, sweetheart."

Yet there was one—not Michael—who, if he lived, must keep me from her, and for whose life I was going forth to stake my own. And his figure—the lithe, buoyant figure I had met in the woods of Zenda—the dull, inert mass I had left in the cellar of the shooting lodge—seemed to rise, double-shaped, before me, and to come between us, thrusting itself in even where she lay, pale, exhausted, fainting, in my arms, and yet looking up at me with those eyes that bore such love as I have never seen, and haunt me now, and will till the ground closes over me—and (who knows?) perhaps beyond.

12

I receive a Visitor and bait a Hook

About five miles from Zenda, on the opposite side from that on which the castle was situated, there lies a large tract of wood. It is rising ground, and in the centre of the demesne, on the top of the hill, stands a fine modern chateau, the property of a distant kinsman of Fritz's, the Count Stanislas von Tarlenheim. Count Stanislas himself was a student and a recluse. He seldom visited the house and had, on Fritz's request, very readily and courteously offered me its hospitality for myself and my party. This, then, was our destination; chosen ostensibly for the sake of the boar hunting (for the wood was carefully preserved, and boars, once common all over Ruritania, were still to be found there in considerable numbers), really because it brought us within striking distance of the Duke of Strelsau's more magnificent dwelling on the other side of the town. A large party of servants, with horses and luggage, started early in the morning. We followed at midday, travelling by train for thirty miles and then mounting our horses to ride the remaining distance to the chateau.

We were a gallant party. Besides Sapt and Fritz, I was accompanied by ten gentlemen. Every one of them had been carefully chosen, and no less carefully sounded by my two friends, and all were devotedly attached to the person of the king. They were told a part of the truth. The attempt on my life in the summerhouse was revealed to them as a spur to their loyalty and an indictment against Michael. They were also informed that a friend of the king's was suspected to be forcibly confined within the castle of Zenda. His rescue was one of the objects of the expedition, but, it was added, the king's main desire was to carry into effect certain steps against his treacherous brother, as to the precise nature of which they could not at present be further enlightened. Enough that the king commanded their services and would rely on their devotion when occasion arose to call for it. Young, well bred, brave, and loyal, they asked no more. They were ready to prove their dutiful obedience and prayed for a fight as the best and most exhilarating mode of showing it.

Thus the scene was shifted from Strelsau to the chateau of Tarlenheim and castle of Zenda which frowned at us across the valley. I tried to shift my thoughts also, to forget my love, and to bend all my energies to the task before me. It was to get the king out of the castle alive. Force was useless: in some trick lay the chance; and I had already an inkling of what we must do. But I was terribly hampered by the publicity which attended my movements. Michael must know by now of my expedition, and I knew Michael too well to suppose that his eyes would be blinded by the feint of the boar hunt. He would understand very well what the real quarry was. That, however, must be risked—that and all it might mean; for Sapt, no less than myself, recognized that the present state of things had become unendurable. And there was one thing that I dared to calculate on—not, as I now know, without warrant. It was this—that Black Michael would not believe that I meant well by the king. He could not appreciate—I will not say an honest man, for the thoughts of my own heart have been revealed—but a man acting honestly. He saw my opportunity as I had seen it, as Sapt had seen it. He knew the princess—nay (and I declare that a sneaking sort of pity for him invaded me), in his way he loved her. He would think that Sapt and Fritz could be bribed, were the bribe large enough. Thinking thus, would he kill the king, my rival and my danger? Aye, verily, that he would, with as little compunction as he would kill a rat. But he would kill Rudolf Rassendyll first, if he could, and nothing but the certainty of being utterly damned by the release of the king alive and his restoration to the throne would drive him to throw away the trump card which he held in reserve to balk the supposed game of the impudent impostor Rassendyll. Musing on all this as I rode along, I took courage.

Michael knew of my coming, sure enough. I had not been in the house an hour when an imposing embassy arrived from him. He did not quite reach the impudence of sending my would-be assassins, but he sent the other three of his famous Six—the three Ruritanian gentlemen—Lauengram, Krafstein, and Rupert Hentzau. A fine, strapping trio they were, splendidly horsed and admirably equipped. Young Rupert, who looked a daredevil and could not have been more than twenty-two or twenty-three, took the lead and made us the neatest speech, wherein my devoted subject and loving brother, Michael of Strelsau, prayed me to pardon him for not paying his addresses in person, and, further, for not putting his castle at my disposal. The reason for both of these apparent derelictions being that he and several of his servants lay sick of scarlet fever, and were in a very sad, and also a very infectious, state. So declared young Rupert with an insolent smile on his curling upper lip and a toss of his thick hair—he was a handsome villain, and the gossip ran that many a lady had troubled her heart for him already.

"If my brother has scarlet fever," said I, "he is nearer my complexion than he is wont to be, my lord. I trust he does not suffer?"

"He is able to attend to his affairs, sire."

"I hope all beneath your roof are not sick. What of my good friends De Gautet, Bersonin, and Detchard? I heard the last had suffered a hurt."

Lauengram and Krafstein looked glum and uneasy, but young Rupert's smile grew broader.

"He hopes soon to find a medicine for it, sire," he answered.

And I burst out laughing, for I knew what medicine Detchard longed for—it is called Revenge.

"You will dine with us, gentlemen?" I asked.

Young Rupert was profuse in apologies. They had urgent duties at the castle.

"Then," said I, with a wave of my hand, "to our next meeting, gentlemen. May it make us better acquainted!"

"We will pray your Majesty for an early opportunity," quoth Rupert airily, and he strode past Sapt with such jeering scorn on his face that I saw the old fellow clench his fist and scowl black as night.

For my part, if a man must needs be a knave I would have him be a debonair knave, and I liked Rupert Hentzau better than his long-faced, close-eyed companions. It makes your sin no worse, as I conceive, to do it *à la mode* and stylishly.

Now it was a curious thing that on this first night, instead of eating the excellent dinner my cooks had prepared for me, I must needs leave my gentlemen to eat it alone, under Sapt's presiding care, and ride myself with Fritz to the town of Zenda and a certain little inn that I knew of. There was little danger in the excursion. The evenings were long and light, and the road this side of Zenda well frequented. So off we rode, with a groom behind us. I muffled myself up in a big cloak.

"Fritz," said I as we entered the town, "there's an uncommonly pretty girl at this inn."

"How do you know?" he asked.

"Because I've been there," said I.

"Since—" he began.

"No. Before," said I.

"But they'll recognize you?"

"Well, of course they will. Now don't argue, my good fellow, but listen to me. We're two gentlemen of the king's household, and one of us has a toothache. The other will order a private room and dinner, and further, a bottle of the best wine for the sufferer. And if he be as clever a fellow as I take him for, the pretty girl and no other will wait on us."

"What if she won't?" objected Fritz.

"My dear Fritz," said I, "if she won't for you she will for me."

We were at the inn. Nothing of me but my eyes was visible as I walked in. The landlady received us; two minutes later my little friend (ever, I fear me, on the lookout for such guests as might prove amusing) made her appearance. Dinner and the wine were ordered. I sat down in the private room. A minute later Fritz came in.

"She's coming," he said.

"If she were not I should have to doubt the Countess Helga's taste."

She came in. I gave her time to set the wine down—I didn't want it dropped. Fritz poured out a glass and gave it to me.

"Is the gentleman in great pain?" the girl asked sympathetically.

"The gentleman is no worse than when he saw you last," said I, throwing away my cloak.

She started with a little shriek. Then she cried: "It was the king, then! I told mother so the minute I saw his picture. Oh, sir, forgive me!"

"Faith, you gave me nothing that hurt much," said I.

"But the things we said!"

"I forgive them for the thing you did."

"I must go and tell mother."

"Stop," said I, assuming a graver air. "We are not here for sport tonight. Go and bring dinner, and not a word of the king being here."

She came back in a few minutes, looking grave, yet very curious.

"Well, how is Johann?" I asked, beginning my dinner.

"Oh, that fellow, sir—my lord king, I mean!"

"'Sir' will do, please. How is he?"

"We hardly see him now, sir."

"And why not?"

"I told him he came too often, sir," said she, tossing her head.

"So he sulks and stays away?"

"Yes, sir."

"But you could bring him back?" I suggested, with a smile.

"Perhaps I could," said she.

"I know your powers, you see," said I, and she blushed with pleasure.

"It's not only that, sir, that keeps him away. He's very busy at the castle now."

"But there's no shooting on now."

"No, sir, but he's in charge of the house."

"Johann turned housemaid?"

The little girl was brimming over with gossip.

"Well, there are no others," said she. "There's not a woman there—not as a servant, I mean. They do say—but perhaps it's false, sir."

"Let's have it for what it's worth," said I.

"Indeed, I'm ashamed to tell you, sir."

"Oh, see, I'm looking at the ceiling."

"They do say there is a lady there, sir, but except for her, there's not a woman in the place. And Johann has to wait on the gentlemen."

"Poor Johann! He must be overworked. Yet I'm sure he could find half an hour to come and see you."

"It would depend on the time, sir, perhaps."

"Do you love him?" I asked.

"Not I, sir."

"And you wish to serve the king?"

"Yes, sir."

"Then tell him to meet you at the second milestone out of Zenda tomorrow evening at ten o'clock. Say you'll be there and will walk home with him."

"Do you mean him harm, sir?"

"Not if he will do as I bid him. But I think I've told you enough, my pretty maid. See that you do as I bid you. And, mind, no one is to know that the king has been here."

I spoke a little sternly, for there is seldom harm in infusing a little fear into a woman's liking for you, and I softened the effect by giving her a handsome present. Then we dined, and wrapping my cloak about my face, with Fritz leading the way, we went downstairs to our horses again.

It was but half-past eight, and hardly yet dark. The streets were full for such a quiet little place, and I could see that gossip was all agog. With the king on one side and the duke on the other, Zenda felt itself the centre of all Ruritania. We jogged gently through the town, but set our horses to a sharper pace when we reached the open country.

"You want to catch this fellow Johann?" asked Fritz.

"Aye, and I fancy I've baited the hook right. Our little Delilah will bring our Samson. It is not enough, Fritz, to have no women in a house, though brother Michael shows some wisdom there. If you want safety you must have none within fifty miles."

"None nearer than Strelsau, for instance," said poor Fritz, with a lovelorn sigh.

We reached the avenue of the chateau and were soon at the house. As the hoofs of our horses sounded on the gravel, Sapt rushed out to meet us.

"Thank God, you're safe!" he cried. "Have you seen anything of them?"

"Of whom?" I asked, dismounting.

He drew us aside, that the grooms might not hear.

"Lad," he said to me, "you must not ride about here unless with half a dozen of us. You know among our men a tall young fellow, Bernenstein by name?"

I knew him. He was a fine, strapping young man, almost of my height and of light complexion.

"He lies in his room upstairs with a bullet through his arm."

"The deuce he does!"

"After dinner he strolled out alone and went a mile or so into the wood; and as he walked he thought he saw three men among the trees; and one levelled a gun at him. He had no weapon, and he started at a run back towards the house. But one of them fired, and he was hit and had much ado to reach here before he fainted. By good luck, they feared to pursue him nearer the house."

He paused, and added, "Lad, the bullet was meant for you."

"It is very likely," said I, "and it's first blood to brother Michael."

"I wonder which three it was," said Fritz.

"Well, Sapt," I said, "I went out tonight for no idle purpose, as you shall hear. But there's one thing in my mind."

"What's that?" he asked.

"Why, this," I answered. "That I shall ill requite the very great honours Ruritania has done me if I depart from it leaving one of those Six alive—neither, with the help of God, will I."

And Sapt shook my hand on that.

13

An Improvement on Jacob's Ladder

In the morning of the day after that on which I swore my oath against the Six, I gave certain orders and then rested in greater contentment than I had known for some time. I was at work; and work, though it cannot cure love, is yet a narcotic to it. So that Sapt, who grew feverish, marvelled to see me sprawling in an armchair in the sunshine, listening to one of my friends who sang me amorous songs in a mellow voice and induced in me a pleasing melancholy. Thus was I engaged when young Rupert Hentzau, who feared neither man nor devil, and rode through the demesne—where every tree might hide a marksman, for all he knew—as though it had been the park of Strelsau, cantered up to where I lay, bowing with burlesque deference and craving private speech with me in order to deliver a message from the Duke of Strelsau. I made all withdraw, and then he said, seating himself by me, "The king is in love, it seems?"

"Not with life, my lord," said I, smiling.

"It is well," he rejoined. "Come, we are alone. Rassendyll—"

I rose to a sitting posture.

"What's the matter?" he asked.

"I was about to call one of my gentlemen to bring your horse, my lord. If you do not know how to address the king, my brother must find another messenger."

"Why keep up the farce?" he asked, negligently dusting his boot with his glove.

"Because it is not finished yet, and meanwhile I'll choose my own name."

"Oh, so be it! Yet I spoke in love for you, for indeed you are a man after my own heart."

"Saving my poor honesty," said I, "maybe I am. But that I keep faith with men, and honour with women, maybe I am, my lord."

He darted a glance at me—a glance of anger.

"Is your mother dead?" said I.

"Aye, she's dead."

"She may thank God," said I, and I heard him curse me softly. "Well, what's the message?" I continued.

I had touched him in the raw, for all the world knew he had broken his mother's heart and flaunted his mistresses in her house, and his airy manner was gone for the moment.

"The duke offers you more than I would," he growled. "A halter for you, sire, was my suggestion. But he offers you safe conduct across the frontier and a million crowns."

"I prefer your offer, my lord, if I am bound to one."

"You refuse?"

"Of course."

"I told Michael you would," and the villain, his temper restored, gave me the sunniest of smiles. "The fact is, between ourselves," he continued, "Michael doesn't understand a gentleman."

I began to laugh.

"And you?" I asked.

"I do," he said. "Well, well, the halter be it."

"I'm sorry you won't live to see it," I observed.

"Has his Majesty done me the honour to fasten a particular quarrel on me?"

"I would you were a few years older, though."

"Oh, God gives years, but the devil gives increase," laughed he. "I can hold my own."

"How is your prisoner?" I asked.

"The k——"

"Your prisoner."

"I forgot your wishes, sire. Well, he is alive."

He rose to his feet. I imitated him. Then, with a smile, he said, "And the pretty princess? Faith, I'll wager the next Elphberg will be red enough, for all that Black Michael will be called his father."

I sprang a step towards him, clenching my hand. He did not move an inch, and his lip curled in insolent amusement.

"Go, while your skin's whole!" I muttered. He had repaid me with interest my hit about his mother.

Then came the most audacious thing I have known in my life. My friends were some thirty yards away. Rupert called to a groom to bring him his horse and dismissed the fellow with a crown. The horse stood near. I stood still, suspecting nothing. Rupert made as though to mount, then he suddenly turned to me, his left hand resting on his belt, his right outstretched:

"Shake hands," he said.

I bowed and did as he had foreseen—I put my hands behind me. Quicker than thought, his left hand darted out at me, and a small dagger flashed in the air; he struck me in the left shoulder— had I not swerved it had been my heart. With a cry I staggered back. Without touching the stirrup, he leaped upon his horse and was off like an arrow, pursued by cries and revolver shots—the last as useless as the first—and I sank into my chair, bleeding profusely, as I watched the devil's brat disappear down the long avenue. My friends surrounded me, and then I fainted.

I suppose that I was put to bed, and there lay unconscious or half conscious for many hours; for it was night when I awoke to my full mind and found Fritz beside me. I was weak and weary, but he bade me be of good cheer, saying that my wound would soon heal and that meanwhile all had gone well, for Johann, the keeper, had fallen into the snare we had laid for him and was even now in the house.

"And the queer thing is," pursued Fritz, "that I fancy he's not altogether sorry to find himself here. He seems to think that when Black Michael has brought off his coup, witnesses of how it was effected—saving, of course, the Six themselves—will not be at a premium."

This idea argued a shrewdness in our captive which led me to build hopes on his assistance. I ordered him to be brought in at once. Sapt conducted him and set him in a chair by my bedside.

He was sullen and afraid, but, to say truth, after young Rupert's exploit we also had our fears, and if he got as far as possible from Sapt's formidable six-shooter, Sapt kept him as far as he could from me. Moreover, when he came in his hands were bound, but that I would not suffer.

I need not stay to recount the safeguards and rewards we promised the fellow—all of which were honourably observed and paid, so that he lives now in prosperity (though where I may not mention), and we were the more free inasmuch as we soon learned that he was rather a weak man than a wicked, and had acted throughout this matter more from fear of the duke and of his own brother Max than for any love of what was done. But he had persuaded all of his loyalty, and though not in their secret counsels, was yet, by his knowledge of their dispositions within the castle, able to lay bare before us the very heart of their devices. And here, in brief is his story:

Below the level of the ground in the castle, approached by a flight of stone steps which abutted on the end of the drawbridge, were situated two small rooms, cut out of the rock itself. The outer of the two had no windows, but was always lighted with candles; the inner had one square window, which gave upon the moat. In this inner room there lay always, day and night, three of the Six; and the instructions of Duke Michael were that on any attack being made on the outer room the three were to defend the door of it so long as they could without risk to themselves. But so soon as the door should be in danger of being forced, then Rupert Hentzau or Detchard (for one of these two was always there) should leave the others to hold it as long as they could and himself pass into the inner room, and without more ado kill the king, who lay there, well treated indeed, but without weapons, and with his arms confined in fine steel chains, which did not allow him to move his elbow more than three inches from his shoulder. Thus before the outer door were stormed the king would be dead. And his body? For his body would be evidence as damning as himself.

"Nay, sir," said Johann, "his Highness has thought of that. While the two hold the outer room the one who has killed the king unlocks the bars in the square window (they turn on a hinge). The window now gives no light, for its mouth is choked by a great pipe of earthenware; and this pipe, which is large enough to let pass through it the body of a man, passes into the moat, coming to an end immediately above the surface of the water, so that there is no perceptible interval between water and pipe. The king being dead, his murderer swiftly ties a weight to the body, and dragging it to the window, raises it by a pulley (for, lest the weight should prove too great, Detchard has provided one) till it is level with the mouth of the pipe. He inserts the feet in the pipe, and pushes the body down. Silently, without splash or sound, it falls into the water and thence to the bottom of the moat, which is twenty feet deep thereabouts. This done, the murderer cries loudly, 'All's well!' and himself slides down the pipe, and the others, if they can and the attack is not too hot, run to the inner room and, seeking a moment's delay, bar the door, and in their turn slide down. And though the king rises not from the bottom, they rise and swim round to the other side, where the orders are for men to await them with ropes, to haul them out, and horses. And here, if things go ill, the duke will join them and seek safety by riding, but if all goes well they will return to the castle and have their enemies in a trap. That, sir, is the plan of his Highness for the disposal of the king in case of need. But it is not to be used till the last; for, as we all know, he is not minded to kill the king unless he can, before or soon after, kill you also, sir. Now, sir, I have spoken the truth, as God is my witness, and I pray you to shield me from the vengeance of Duke Michael; for if, after he knows what I have done, I fall into his hands, I shall pray for one thing out of all the world—a speedy death, and that I shall not obtain from him!"

The fellow's story was rudely told, but our questions supplemented his narrative. What he had told us applied to an armed attack, but if suspicions were aroused and there came overwhelming force—such, for instance, as I, the king, could bring—the idea of resistance would be abandoned. The king would be quietly murdered and slid down the pipe. And—here comes an ingenious touch—one of the Six would take his place in the cell, and on the entrance of the searchers loudly demand release and redress; and Michael, being summoned, would confess to hasty action, but he would say the man had angered him by seeking the favour of a lady in the castle (this was Antoinette de Mauban), and he had confined him there, as he conceived he, as Lord of Zenda, had right to do. But he was now, on receiving his apology, content to let him go, and so end the gossip which, to his Highness's annoyance, had arisen concerning a prisoner of Zenda and had given his visitors the trouble of his inquiry. The visitors, baffled, would retire, and Michael could, at his leisure, dispose of the body of the king.

Sapt, Fritz, and I in my bed looked round on one another in horror and bewilderment at the cruelty and cunning of the plan. Whether I went in peace or in war, openly at the head of a corps, or secretly by a stealthy assault, the king would be dead before I could come near him. If Michael were stronger and overcame my party there would be an end. But if I were stronger I should have no way to punish him, no means of proving any guilt in him without proving my own guilt also. On the other hand, I should be left as king (ah! for a moment my pulse quickened), and it would be for the future to witness the final struggle between him and me. He seemed to have made triumph possible and ruin impossible. At the worst he would stand where he had stood before I crossed his path—with but one man between him and the throne, and that man an impostor. At best there would be none left to stand against him. I had begun to think that Black Michael was overfond of leaving the fighting to his friends, but now I acknowledged that the brains, if not the arms, of the conspiracy were his.

"Does the king know this?" I asked.

"I and my brother," answered Johann, "put up the pipe under the orders of my Lord of Hentzau. He was on guard that day, and the king asked my lord what it meant. 'Faith,' he answered, with his airy laugh, 'it's a new improvement on the ladder of Jacob, whereby, as you have read, sire, men pass from earth to heaven. We thought it not meet that your Majesty should go, in case, sire, you must go, by the common route. So we have made you a pretty private passage, where the vulgar cannot stare at you or incommode your passage. That, sire, is the meaning of that pipe.' And he laughed and bowed, and prayed the king's leave to replenish the king's glass—for the king was at supper. And the king, though he is a brave man, as are all of his House, grew red and then white as he looked on the pipe and at the merry devil who mocked him. Ah, sir,"—and the fellow shuddered—"it is not easy to sleep quiet in the castle of Zenda, for all of them would as soon cut a man's throat as play a game at cards; and my Lord Rupert would choose it sooner for a pastime than any other—aye, sooner than he would ruin a woman, though that he loves also."

The man ceased, and I bade Fritz take him away and have him carefully guarded; and, turning to him, I added, "If anyone asks you if there is a prisoner in Zenda you may answer 'Yes'. But if any asks who the prisoner is, do not answer. For all my promises will not save you if any man here learns from you the truth as to the prisoner in Zenda. I'll kill you like a dog if the thing be so much as breathed within the house!"

Then when he was gone I looked at Sapt.

"It is a hard nut!" said I.

"So hard," said he, shaking his grizzled head, "that, as I think, this time next year is like to find you still King of Ruritania!" and he broke out into curses on Michael's cunning.

I lay back on my pillows.

"There seems to me," I observed, "to be two ways by which the king can come out of Zenda alive. One is by treachery in the duke's followers."

"You can leave that out," said Sapt.

"I hope not," I rejoined, "because the other I was about to mention is—by a miracle from Heaven!"

14

A Night outside the Castle

It would have surprised the good people of Ruritania to know of
the foregoing talk, for according to the official reports I had suffered a grievous and dangerous hurt from an accidental spear
thrust received in the course of my sport. I caused the bulletins to
be of a very serious character, and created great public excitement, whereby three things occurred: first, I gravely offended the
medical faculty of Strelsau by refusing to summon to my bedside
any of them save a young man, a friend of Fritz's, whom we
could trust; secondly, I received word from Marshal Strakencz
that my orders seemed to have no more weight than his, and that
the Princess Flavia was leaving for Tarlenheim under his unwilling escort (news whereat I strove not to be glad and proud); and
thirdly, my brother, the Duke of Strelsau, although too well informed to believe the account of the origin of my sickness, was
yet persuaded by the reports and by my seeming inactivity that I
was in truth incapable of action, and that my life was in some
danger. This I learned from the man Johann, whom I was compelled to trust and send back to Zenda, where, by the way, Rupert
Hentzau had him soundly flogged for daring to smirch the morals
of Zenda by staying out all night in the pursuits of love. This,
from Rupert, Johann deeply resented, and the duke's approval of
it did more to bind the keeper to my side than all my promises.

On Flavia's arrival I cannot dwell. Her joy at finding me up and
well, instead of on my back and fighting with death, makes a picture that even now dances before my eyes till they grow too dim
to see it; and her reproaches that I had not trusted even her must

excuse the means I took to quiet them. In truth, to have her with me once more was like a taste of heaven to a damned soul, the sweeter for the inevitable doom that was to follow; and I rejoiced in being able to waste two whole days with her. And when I had wasted two days the Duke of Strelsau arranged a hunting party.

The stroke was near now. For Sapt and I, after anxious consultations, had resolved that we must risk a blow, our resolution being clinched by Johann's news that the king grew peaked, pale, and ill, and that his health was breaking down under his rigorous confinement. Now a man—be he king or no king—may as well die swiftly, and as becomes a gentleman, from bullet or thrust, as rot his life out in a cellar! That thought made prompt action advisable in the interests of the king; from my own point of view it grew more and more necessary. For Strakencz urged on me the need of a speedy marriage, and my own inclinations seconded him with such terrible insistence that I feared for my resolution. I do not believe that I should have done the deed I dreamt of, but I might have come to flight, and my flight would have ruined the cause. And—yes, I am no saint (ask my little sister-in-law), and worse still might have happened.

It is perhaps as strange a thing as has ever been in the history of a country that the king's brother and the king's personator, in a time of profound outward peace, near a placid, undisturbed country town, under semblance of amity, should wage a desperate war for the person and life of the king. Yet such was the struggle that began now between Zenda and Tarlenheim. When I look back on the time I seem to myself to have been half mad. Sapt has told me that I suffered no interference and listened to no remonstrances; and if ever a King of Ruritania ruled like a despot I was, in those days, the man. Look where I would I saw nothing that made life sweet to me, and I took my life in my hand and carried it carelessly as a man dangles an old glove. At first they strove to guard me, to keep me safe, to persuade me not to expose myself; but when they saw how I was set there grew up among them— whether they knew the truth or not—a feeling that Fate ruled the issue and that I must be left to play my game with Michael my own way.

Late next night I rose from table, where Flavia had sat by me, and conducted her to the door of her apartments. There I kissed her hand and bade her sleep sound and wake to happy days. Then I changed my clothes and went out. Sapt and Fritz were waiting for me with three men and the horses. Over his saddle Sapt carried a long coil of rope, and both were heavily armed. I had with me a short stout cudgel and a long knife. Making a circuit, we avoided the town and in an hour found ourselves slowly mounting the hill that led to the castle of Zenda. The night was dark and very stormy; gusts of wind and spits of rain caught us as we breasted the incline, and the great trees moaned and sighed. When we came to a thick clump, about a quarter of a mile from the castle, we bade our three friends hide there with the horses. Sapt had a whistle, and they could rejoin us in a few moments if danger came, but up till now we had met no one. I hoped that Michael was still off his guard, believing me to be safe in bed. However that might be, we gained the top of the hill without accident and found ourselves on the edge of the moat where it sweeps under the road, separating the old castle from it. A tree stood on the edge of the bank, and Sapt silently and diligently set to make fast the rope. I stripped off my boots, took a pull at a flask of brandy, loosened the knife in its sheath, and took the cudgel between my teeth. Then I shook hands with my friends, not heeding a last look of entreaty from Fritz, and laid hold of the rope. I was going to have a look at Jacob's ladder.

Gently I lowered myself into the water. Though the night were wild, the day had been warm and bright, and the water was not cold. I struck out and began to swim round the great walls which frowned above me. I could see only three yards ahead. I had then good hopes of not being seen, as I crept along close under the damp, moss-grown masonry. There were lights from the new part of the castle on the other side, and now and again I heard laughter and merry shouts. I fancied I recognized young Rupert Hentzau's ringing tones and pictured him flushed with wine. Recalling my thoughts to the business at hand, I rested a moment. If Johann's description were right I must be near the window now. Very slowly I moved, and out of the darkness ahead loomed a shape. It was the pipe, curving from the window to the water. About two feet of its surface was displayed; it was as big round as two men. I was about to approach it when I saw something else, and my heart stood still. The nose of a boat protruded beyond the pipe on the other side; and listening intently, I heard a slight shuffle—as of a man shifting his position. Who was the man who guarded Michael's invention? Was he awake or was he asleep? I felt if my knife were ready, and trod water. As I did so, I found bottom under my feet. The foundations of the castle extended some fifteen inches, making a ledge; and I stood on it, out of water from my armpits upwards. Then I crouched and peered through the darkness under the pipe, where, curving, it left a space.

There was a man in the boat. A rifle lay by him—I saw the gleam of the barrel. Here was the sentinel! He sat very still. I listened: he breathed heavily, regularly, monotonously. By Heaven, he slept! Kneeling on the shelf, I drew forwards under the pipe till my face was within two feet of his. He was a big man, I saw. It was Max Holf, the brother of Johann. My hand stole to my belt, and I drew out my knife. Of all the deeds of my life I love the least to think of this, and whether it was the act of a man or a traitor I will not ask. I said to myself: "It is war—and the king's life is the stake." And I raised myself from beneath the pipe and stood up by the boat, which lay moored by the ledge. Holding my breath, I marked the spot and raised my arm. The great fellow stirred. He opened his eyes—wide, wider. He gasped in terror at my face and clutched at his rife. I struck home. And I heard the chorus of a love song from the opposite bank.

Leaving him where he lay, a huddled mass, I turned to "Jacob's ladder". My time was short. This fellow's turn of watching might be over directly, and relief would come. Leaning over the pipe, I examined it, from the point it left the water to the topmost extremity where it passed, or seemed to pass, through the masonry of the wall. There was no break in it, no chink. Dropping on my knees, I tested the under side. And my breath went quick and fast, for on this lower side, where the pipe should have clung close to the masonry, there was a gleam of light! That light must come from the cell of the king! I set my shoulder against the pipe and exerted my strength. The chink widened a very, very little, and hastily I desisted; I had done enough to show that the pipe was not fixed in the masonry at the lower side.

Then I heard a voice—a harsh, grating voice: "Well, sire, if you have had enough of my society I will leave you to repose, but I must fasten the little ornaments first."

It was Detchard! I caught the English accent in a moment.

"Have you anything to ask, sire, before we part?"

The king's voice followed. It was his, though it was faint and hollow—different from the merry tones I had heard in the glades of the forest.

"Pray my brother," said the king, "to kill me. I am dying by inches here."

"The duke does not desire your death, sire—yet," sneered Detchard. "When he does, behold your path to heaven!"

The king answered: "So be it! And now, if your orders allow it, pray leave me.

"May you dream of paradise!" said the ruffian.

The light disappeared. I heard the bolts of the door run home. And then I heard the sobs of the king. He was alone, as he thought. Who dares mock at him?

I did not venture to speak to him. The risk of some exclamation escaping him in surprise was too great. I dared do nothing that night, and my task now was to get myself away in safety and to carry off the carcass of the dead man. To leave him there would tell too much. Casting loose the boat, I got in. The wind was blowing a gale now, and there was little danger of oars being heard. I rowed swiftly round to where my friends waited. I had just reached the spot when a loud whistle sounded over the moat behind me.

"Hullo, Max!" I heard shouted.

I hailed Sapt in a low tone. The rope came down. I tied it round the corpse, and then went up it myself.

"Whistle you, too," I whispered, "for our men and haul in the line. No talk now."

They hauled up the body. Just as it reached the road, three men on horseback swept round from the front of the castle. We saw them, but, being on foot ourselves, we escaped their notice. But we heard our men coming up with a shout,

"The devil, but it's dark!" cried a ringing voice.

It was young Rupert. A moment later shots rang out. Our people had met them. I started forwards at a run, Sapt and Fritz following me.

"Thrust, thrust!" cried Rupert again, and a loud groan following told that he himself was not behindhand.

"I'm done, Rupert!" cried a voice. "They're three to one. Save yourself!"

I ran on, holding my cudgel in my hand. Suddenly a horse came towards me. A man was on it, leaning over the shoulder.

"Are you cooked too, Krafstein?" he cried.

There was no answer.

I sprang to the horse's head. It was Rupert Hentzau.

"At last!" I cried.

For we seemed to have him. He had only his sword in his hand. My men were hot upon him; Sapt and Fritz were running up, I had outstripped them; but if they got close enough to fire he must die or surrender.

"At last!" I cried.

"It's the play-actor!" cried he, slashing at my cudgel. He cut it clean in two; and, judging discretion better than death, I ducked my head and (I blush to tell) scampered for my life. The devil was in Rupert Hentzau, for he put spurs to his horse, and I, turning to look, saw him ride, full gallop, to the edge of the moat and leap in, while the shots of our party fell thick round him like hail. With one gleam of moonlight we should have riddled him with balls, but in the darkness he won to the corner of the castle and vanished from our sight.

"The deuce take him!" grinned Sapt.

"It's a pity," said I, "that he's a villain. Whom have we got?"

We had Lauengram and Krafstein. They lay stiff and dead; and, concealment being no longer possible, we flung them, with Max, into the moat; and, drawing together in a compact body, rode off down the hill. And in our midst went the bodies of four gallant gentlemen. Thus we travelled home, heavy at heart for the death of our friends, sore uneasy concerning the king, and cut to the quick that young Rupert had played yet another winning hand with us.'

For my own part I was vexed and angry that I had killed no man in open fight but only stabbed a knave in his sleep. And I did not love to hear Rupert call me a play-actor.

15

I talk with a Tempter

Ruritania is not England, or the quarrel between Duke Michael and myself could not have gone on, with the remarkable incidents which marked it, without more public notice being directed to it. Duels were frequent among all the upper classes, and private quarrels between great men kept the old habit of spreading to their friends and dependants. Nevertheless, after the affray which I have just related, such reports began to circulate that I felt it necessary to be on my guard. The death of the gentlemen involved could not be hidden from their relatives. I issued a stern order, declaring that duelling had attained unprecedented licence (the chancellor drew up the document for me, and very well he did it) and forbidding it save in the gravest cases. I sent a public and stately apology to Michael, and he returned a deferential and courteous reply to me; for our one point of union was—and it underlay all our differences and induced an unwilling harmony between our actions—that we could neither of us afford to throw our cards on the table. He, as well as I, was a "play-actor", and, hating one another, we combined to dupe public opinion. Unfortunately, however, the necessity for concealment involved the necessity of delay: the king might die in his prison, or even be spirited off somewhere else, it could not be helped. For a little while I was compelled to observe a truce, and my only consolation was that Flavia most warmly approved of my edict against duelling; and when I expressed delight at having won her favour, prayed me, if her favour were any motive to me, to prohibit the practice altogether.

"Wait till we are married," said I, smiling.

Not the least peculiar result of the truce and of the secrecy which dictated it was that the town of Zenda became in the day-time—I would not have trusted far to its protection by night—a sort of neutral zone, where both parties could safely go; and I, riding down one day with Flavia and Sapt, had an encounter with an acquaintance, which presented a ludicrous side but was at the same time embarrassing. As I rode along I met a dignified-looking person driving in a two-horsed carriage. He stopped his horses, got out, and approached me, bowing low. I recognized the head of the Strelsau police.

"Your Majesty's ordinance as to duelling is receiving our best attention," he assured me.

If the best attention involved his presence in Zenda I determined at once to dispense with it.

"Is that what brings you to Zenda, prefect?" I asked.

"Why, no, sire. I am here because I desired to oblige the British ambassador."

"What's the British ambassador doing *dans cette galère*?" said I carelessly.

"A young countryman of his, sire—a man of some position—is missing. His friends have not heard from him for two months, and there is reason to believe that he was last seen in Zenda."

Flavia was paying little attention. I dared not look at Sapt.

"What reason?"

"A friend of his in Paris—a certain M. Featherly—has given us information which makes it possible that he came here, and the officials of the railway recollect his name on some luggage."

"What was his name?"

"Rassendyll, sire," he answered, and I saw that the name meant nothing to him. But, glancing at Flavia, he lowered his voice as he went on, "It is thought that he may have followed a lady here. Has your Majesty heard of a certain Mme de Mauban?"

"Why, yes," said I, my eye involuntarily travelling towards the castle. "She arrived in Ruritania about the same time as this Rassendyll."

I caught the prefect's glance. He was regarding me with inquiry writ large on his face.

"Sapt," said I, "I must speak a word to the prefect. Will you ride on a few paces with the princess?" And I added to the prefect, "Come, sir, what do you mean?"

He drew close to me, and I bent in the saddle.

"If he were in love with the lady?" he whispered. "Nothing has been heard of him for two months," and this time it was the eye of the prefect which travelled towards the castle.

"Yes, the lady is there," I said quietly. "But I don't suppose Mr Rassendyll—is that the name?—is."

"The duke," he whispered, "does not like rivals, sire."

"You're right there," said I, with all sincerity. "But surely you hint at a very grave charge."

He spread his hands out in apology. I whispered in his ear, "This is a grave matter. Go back to Strelsau—"

"But, sire, if I have a clue here?"

"Go back to Strelsau," I repeated. "Tell the ambassador that you have a clue but that you must be left alone for a week or two. Meanwhile I'll charge myself with looking into the matter."

"The ambassador is very pressing, sire."

"You must quiet him. Come, sir. You see that if your suspicions are correct it is an affair in which we must move with caution. We can have no scandal. Mind you return tonight."

He promised to obey me, and I rode on to rejoin my companions, a little easier in my mind. Inquiries after me must be stopped at all hazards for a week or two, and this clever official had come surprisingly near the truth. His impression might be useful some day, but if he acted on it now it might mean the worst to the king. Heartily did I curse George Featherly for not holding his tongue.

"Well," asked Flavia, "have you finished your business?"

"Most satisfactorily," said I. "Come, shall we turn round? We are almost trenching on my brother's territory."

We were, in fact, at the extreme end of the town, just where the hill begins to mount towards the castle. We cast our eyes up, admiring the massive beauty of the old walls, and we saw a cortege winding slowly down the hill. On it came.

"Let us go back," said Sapt.

"I should like to stay," said Flavia, and I reined my horse beside hers.

We could distinguish the approaching party now. There came first two mounted servants in black uniforms, relieved only by a silver badge. These were followed by a car drawn by four horses. On it, under a heavy pall, lay a coffin. Behind it rode a man in plain black clothes, carrying his hat in his hand. Sapt uncovered, and we stood waiting, Flavia keeping by me and laying her hand on my arm.

"It is one of the gentlemen killed in the quarrel, I expect," she said.

I beckoned to a groom.

"Ride and ask whom they escort," I ordered.

He rode up to the servants, and I saw him pass on to the gentleman who rode behind.

"It's Rupert of Hentzau," whispered Sapt.

Rupert it was, and directly afterwards, waving to the procession to stand still, Rupert trotted up to me. He was in a frock coat, tightly buttoned, and trousers. He wore an aspect of sadness, and he bowed with profound respect. Yet suddenly he smiled, and I smiled too, for old Sapt's hand lay in his left breast pocket, and Rupert and I both guessed what lay in the hand inside the pocket.

"Your Majesty asks whom we escort," said Rupert. "It is my dear friend Albert of Laurengram."

"Sir," said I, "no one regrets the unfortunate affair more than I. My ordinance, which I mean to have obeyed, is witness to it."

"Poor fellow!" said Flavia softly, and I saw Rupert's eyes flash at her. Whereat I grew red, for if I had my way Rupert Hentzau should not have defiled her by so much as a glance. Yet he did it and dared to let admiration be seen in his look.

"Your Majesty's words are gracious," he said. "I grieve for my friend. Yet, sire, others must soon lie as he lies now."

"It is a thing we all do well to remember, my lord," I rejoined.

"Even kings, sire," said Rupert in a moralizing tone, and old Sapt swore softly by my side.

"It is true," said I. "How fares my brother, my lord?"

"He is better, sire."

"I am rejoiced."

"He hopes soon to leave for Strelsau, when his health is secured."

"He is only convalescent, then?"

"There remain one or two small troubles," answered the insolent fellow in the mildest tone in the world.

"Express my earnest hope, said Flavia, "that they may soon
cease to trouble him."

"Your Royal Highness's wish is, humbly, my own," said Rupert
with a bold glance that brought a blush to Flavia's cheek.

I bowed, and Rupert, bowing lower, backed his horse and
signed to his party to proceed. With a sudden impulse I rode after
him. He turned swiftly, fearing that even in the presence of the
dead and before a lady's eyes I meant mischief.

"You fought as a brave man the other night," I said. "Come,
you are young, sir. If you will deliver your prisoner alive to me
you shall come to no hurt."

He looked at me with a mocking smile, but suddenly he rode
nearer to me.

"I'm unarmed," he said, "and our old Sapt there could pick me
off in a minute."

"I'm not afraid," said I.

"No, curse you!" he answered. "Look here, I made you a pro-
posal from the duke once."

"I'll hear nothing from Black Michael," said I.

"Then hear one from me." He lowered his voice to a whisper.
"Attack the castle boldly. Let Sapt and Tarlenheim lead."

"Go on," said I.

"Arrange the time with me."

"I have such confidence in you, my lord!"

"Tut! I'm talking business now. Sapt there and Fritz will fall.
Black Michael will fall—"

"What!"

"Black Michael will fall, like the dog he is. The prisoner, as you
call him, will go by Jacob's ladder—ah, you know what?—to
hell! Two men will be left—I, Rupert Hentzau, and you, the King
of Ruritania."

He paused, and then, in a voice that quivered with eagerness, added, "Isn't that a hand to play?—a throne and yon princess! And for me, say a competence and your Majesty's gratitude."

"Surely," I exclaimed, "while you're above ground hell wants its master!"

"Well, think it over," he said. "And, look you, it would take more than a scruple or two to keep me from yonder girl," and his evil eye flashed again at her I loved.

"Get out of my reach!" said I, and yet in a moment I began to laugh for the very audacity of it.

"Would you turn against your master?" I asked.

He swore at Michael for being what the offspring of a legal, though morganatic, union should not be called, and said to me in an almost confidential and apparently friendly tone, "He gets in my way, you know. He's a jealous brute! Faith, I nearly stuck a knife into him last night; he came most cursedly *mal à propos!*"

My temper was well under control now. I was learning something.

"A lady?" I asked negligently.

"Aye, and a beauty," he nodded. "But you've seen her."

"Ah! Was it at a tea party when some of your friends got on the wrong side of the table?"

"What can you expect of fools like Detchard and De Gautet? I wish I'd been there."

"And the duke interferes?"

"Well," said Rupert meditatively, "that's hardly a fair way of putting it, perhaps. I want to interfere."

"And she prefers the duke?"

"Aye, the silly creature! Ah, well, you think about my plan," and with a bow he pricked his horse and trotted after the body of his friend.

I went back to Flavia and Sapt, pondering on the strangeness of the man. Wicked men I have known in plenty, but Rupert Hentzau remains unique in my experience. And if there be another anywhere let him be caught and hanged out of hand. So say I!

"He's very handsome, isn't he?" said Flavia.

Well, of course she didn't know him as I did, yet I was put out, for I thought his bold glances would have made her angry. But my dear Flavia was a woman, and so—she was not put out. On the contrary, she thought young Rupert was very handsome—as, beyond question, the ruffian was.

"And how sad he looked at his friend's death!" said she.

"He'll have better reason to be sad at his own," observed Sapt with a grim smile.

As for me, I grew sulky. Unreasonable it was, perhaps, for what better business had I to look at her with love than had even Rupert's lustful eyes? And sulky I remained till, as evening fell and we rode up to Tarlenheim, Sapt having fallen behind in case anyone should be following us, Flavia, riding close beside me, said softly, with a little half-ashamed laugh, "Unless you smile, Rudolf, I cry. Why are you angry?"

"It was something that fellow said to me," said I, but I was smiling as we reached the doors and dismounted.

There a servant handed me a note; it was unaddressed.

"Is it for me?" I asked.

"Yes, sir; a boy brought it."

I tore it open:

Johann carries this for me. I warned you once. In the name of God, and if you are a man, rescue me from this den of murderers!

                                                                    A. de M.

I handed it to Sapt, but all that the tough old soul said in reply to this piteous appeal was: "Whose fault brought her there?"

Nevertheless, not being faultless myself, I took leave to pity Antoinette de Mauban.

16

A Desperate Plan

As I had ridden publicly in Zenda and had talked there with
Rupert Hentzau, of course all pretence of illness was at an end. I
marked the effect on the garrison of Zenda. They ceased to be
seen abroad, and any of my men who went near the castle re-
ported that the utmost vigilance prevailed there. Touched as I was
by Mme de Mauban's appeal, I seemed as powerless to befriend
her as I had proved to help the king. Michael bade me defiance,
and—although he too had been seen outside the walls—with
more disregard for appearances than he had hitherto shown, he
did not take the trouble to send any excuse for his failure to wait
on the king. Time ran on in inactivity, when every moment was
pressing, for not only was I faced with the new danger which the
stir about my own disappearance brought on me, but great murmurs had arisen in Strelsau at my continued absence from the
city. They had been greater but for the knowledge that Flavia was
with me, and for this reason I suffered her to stay, though I hated
to have her where danger was and though every day of our
present sweet intercourse strained my endurance almost to breaking. As a final blow nothing would content my advisers,
Strakencz and the chancellor (who came out from Strelsau to
make an urgent representation to me), save that I should appoint a
day for the public solemnization of my betrothal, a ceremony
which in Ruritania is well nigh as binding and great a thing as the
marriage itself. And this—with Flavia sitting by me—I was
forced to do, setting a date a fortnight ahead and appointing the
cathedral in Strelsau as the place. And this formal act, being published far and wide, caused great joy throughout the kingdom and

was the talk of all tongues, so that I reckoned there were but two men who chafed at it—I mean Black Michael and myself; and but one who did not know of it—that one the man whose name I bore, the King of Ruritania.

In truth, I heard something of the way the news was received in the castle, for after an interval of three days the man Johann, greedy for more money though fearful for his life, again found means to visit us. He had been waiting on the duke when the tidings came. Black Michael's face had grown blacker still, and he had sworn savagely. Nor was he better pleased when young Rupert took oath that I meant to do as I said, and turning to Mme de Mauban, wished her joy on a rival gone. Michael's hand stole towards his sword (said Johann), but not a bit did Rupert care, for he rallied the duke on having made a better king than had reigned for years past in Ruritania. "And," said he, with a meaning bow to his exasperated master, "the devil sends the princess a finer man than Heaven had marked out for her. By my soul, he does!" Then Michael harshly bade him hold his tongue and leave them, but Rupert must needs first kiss madame's hand, which he did as though he loved her while Michael glared at him.

This was the lighter side of the fellow's news, but more serious came behind, and it was plain that if time pressed at Tarlenheim it pressed none the less fiercely at Zenda. For the king was very sick. Johann had seen him, and he was wasted and hardly able to move. "There could be no thought of taking another for him now." So alarmed were they that they had sent for a physician from Strelsau; and the physician having been introduced into the king's cell, had come forth pale and trembling, and urgently prayed the duke to let him go back and meddle no more in the affair; but the duke would not and held him there a prisoner, telling him his life was safe if the king lived while the duke desired and died when the duke desired—not otherwise. And, persuaded by the physician, they had allowed Mme de Mauban to visit the king and give him such attendance as his state needed and as only a woman can give. Yet his life hung in the balance, and I was yet strong and whole and free. Wherefore great gloom reigned at Zenda, and save when they quarrelled, to which they were very prone, they hardly spoke. But the deeper the depression of the rest, young Rupert went about Satan's work with a smile in his eye and a song on his lip, and laughed "fit to burst" (said Johann) because the duke always set Detchard to guard the king when Mme de Mauban was in the cell—which precaution was, indeed, not unwise in my careful brother. Thus Johann told his tale and seized his crowns. Yet he besought us to allow him to stay with us in Tarlenheim and not venture his head again in the lion's den, but we had need of him there, and although I refused to constrain him, I prevailed on him by increased rewards to go back and to carry tidings to Mme de Mauban that I was working for her and that, if she could, she should speak one word of comfort to the king. For while suspense is bad for the sick, yet despair is worse still, and it might be that the king lay dying of mere hopelessness, for I could learn of no definite disease that afflicted him.

"And how do they guard the king now?" I asked, remembering that two of the Six were dead, and Max Holf also.

"Detchard and Bersonin watch by night, Rupert Hentzau and Gautet by day, sir," he answered.

"Only two at a time?"

"Aye, sir, but the others rest in a room just above and are within sound of a cry or a whistle."

"A room just above? I didn't know of that. Is there any communication between it and the room where they watch?"

"No, sir. You must go down a few stairs and through the door by the drawbridge, and so to where the king is lodged."

"And that door is locked?"

"Only the four lords have keys, sir."

I drew nearer to him.

"And have they keys of the grating?" I asked in a low whisper.

"I think, sir, only Detchard and Rupert."

"Where does the duke lodge?"

"In the chateau, on the first floor. His apartments are on the right as you go towards the drawbridge."

"And Mme de Mauban?"

"Just opposite, on the left. But her door is locked after she has entered."

"To keep her in?"

"Doubtless, sir."

"Perhaps for another reason?"

"It is possible."

"And the duke, I suppose, has the key?"

"Yes. And the drawbridge is drawn back at night, and of that too the duke holds the key, so that it cannot be run across the moat without application to him."

"And where do you sleep?"

"In the entrance hall of the chateau, with five servants."

"Armed?"

"They have pikes, sir, but no firearms. The duke will not trust them with firearms."

Then at last I took the matter boldly in my hands. I had failed once at Jacob's ladder. I should fail again there. I must make the attack from the other side.

"I have promised you twenty thousand crowns," said I. "You shall have fifty thousand if you will do what I ask of you tomorrow night. But, first, do those servants know who your prisoner is?"

"No, sir. They believe him to be some private enemy of the duke's."

"And they would not doubt that I am the king?"

"How should they?" he asked.

"Look to this, then. Tomorrow, at two in the morning exactly, fling open the front door of the chateau. Don't fail by an instant."

"Shall you be there, sir?"

"Ask no questions. Do what I tell you. Say the hall is closed, or what you will. That is all I ask of you."

"And may I escape by the door, sir, when I have opened it?"

"Yes, as quick as your legs will carry you. One thing more. Carry this note to madame—oh, it's in French, you can't read it— and charge her, for the sake of all our lives, not to fail in what it orders."

The man was trembling, but I had to trust to what he had of courage and to what he had of honesty. I dared not wait, for I feared that the king would die.

When the fellow was gone, I called Sapt and Fritz to me and unfolded the plan that I had formed. Sapt shook his head over it.

"Why can't you wait?" he asked.

"The king may die."

"Michael will be forced to act before that."

"Then," said I, "the king may live."

"Well, and if he does?"

"For a fortnight?" I asked simply.

And Sapt bit his moustache.

Suddenly Fritz von Tarlenheim laid his hand on my shoulder.

"Let us go and make the attempt," said he.

"I mean you to go—don't be afraid," said I.

"Aye, but do you stay here and take care of the princess?"

A gleam came into old Sapt's eye.

"We should have Michael one way or the other then," he chuckled, "whereas if you go and are killed with the king what will become of those of us who are left?"

"They will serve Queen Flavia," said I, "and I would to God I could be one of them."

A pause followed. Old Sapt broke it by saying sadly, yet with an unmeant drollery that set Fritz and me laughing, "Why didn't old Rudolf the Third marry your—great-grand mother, was it?"

"Come," said I, "it is the king we are thinking about."

"It is true," said Fritz.

"Moreover," I went on, "I have been an impostor for the profit of another, but I will not be one for my own; and if the king is not alive and on his throne before the day of betrothal comes I will tell the truth, come what may."

"You shall go, lad," said Sapt.

Here is the plan I had made: A strong party under Sapt's command was to steal up to the door of the chateau. If discovered prematurely they were to kill anyone who found them—with their swords, for I wanted no noise of firing. If all went well they would be at the door when Johann opened it. They were to rush in and secure the servants, if their mere presence and the use of the king's name were not enough. At the same moment—and on this hinged the plan—a woman's cry was to ring out loud and shrill

from Antoinette de Mauban's chamber. Again and again she was
to cry: "Help, help! Michael, help!" and then to utter the name of
young Rupert Hentzau. Then, as we hoped, Michael, in fury,
would rush out of his apartments opposite and fall alive into the
hands of Sapt. Still the cries would go on. My men would let
down the drawbridge, and it would be strange if Rupert, hearing
his name thus taken in vain, did not descend from where he slept
and seek to cross. De Gautet might or might not come with him:
that must be left to chance.

And when Rupert set his foot on the drawbridge? There was my
part, for I was minded for another swim in the moat; and, lest I
should grow weary, I had resolved to take with me a small
wooden ladder on which I could rest my arms in the water—and
my feet when I left it. I would rear it against the wall just by the
bridge, and when the bridge was across I would stealthily creep
on to it—and then if Rupert or De Gautet crossed in safety it
would be my misfortune, not my fault. They dead, two men only
would remain, and for them we must trust to the confusion we
had created and to a sudden rush. We should have the keys of the
door that led to the all-important rooms. Perhaps they would rush
out. If they stood by their orders, then the king's life hung on the
swiftness with which we could force the outer door; and I thanked
God that not Rupert Hentzau watched, but Detchard. For though
Detchard was a cool man, relentless and no coward, he had neither the dash nor the recklessness of Rupert. Moreover, he, if any
one of them, really loved Black Michael, and it might be that he
would leave Bersonin to guard the king and rush across the bridge
to take part in the affray on the other side.

So I planned—desperately. And, that our enemy might be the
better lulled to security, I gave orders that our residence should be
brilliantly lighted from top to bottom, as though we were engaged
in revelry, and should so be kept all night, with music playing and
people moving to and fro. Strakencz would be there, and he was
to conceal our departure, if he could, from Flavia. And if we came
not again by the morning he was to march, openly and in force, to
the castle and demand the person of the king: if Black Michael
were not there, as I did not think he would be, the marshal would

take Flavia with him, as swiftly as he could, to Strelsau, and there proclaim Black Michael's treachery and the probable death of the king, and rally all that there were honest and true round the banner of the princess. And, to say the truth, this was what I thought most likely to happen.

For I had great doubts whether either the king or Black Michael or I had more than a day to live. Well, if Black Michael died, and if I, the play-actor, slew Rupert Hentzau with my own hand and then died myself, it might be that Fate would deal as lightly with Ruritania as could be hoped, notwithstanding that it demanded the life of the king—and to her dealing thus with me I was in no temper to make objection.

It was late when we rose from conference, and I betook me to the princess's apartments. She was pensive that evening, yet when I left her she flung her arms about me and grew, for an instant, bashfully radiant as she slipped a ring on my finger. I was wearing the king's ring, but I had also on my little finger a plain band of gold engraved with the motto of our family, *"Nil Quae Feci"* This I took off and put on her finger and signed to her to let me go. And she, understanding, stood away and watched me with dimmed eyes.

"Wear this ring, even though you wear another when you are queen," I said.

"Whatever else I wear this I will wear till I die, and after," said she as she kissed the ring.

17

Young Rupert's Midnight Diversions

The night came fine and clear. I had prayed for dirty weather, such as had favoured my previous voyage in the moat, but Fortune was this time against me. Still I reckoned that by keeping close under the wall and in the shadow I could escape detection from the windows of the chateau that looked out on the scene of my efforts. If they searched the moat, indeed my scheme must fail, but I did not think they would. They had made Jacob's ladder secure against attack. Johann had himself helped to fix it closely to the masonry on the underside so that it could not now be moved from below any more than from above. An assault with explosives or a long battering with picks alone could displace it, and the noise involved in either of these operations put them out of the question. What harm, then, could a man do in the moat? I trusted that Black Michael, putting this query to himself, would answer confidently, "None," while even if Johann meant treachery he did not know my scheme and would doubtless expect to see me, at the head of my friends, before the front entrance to the chateau. There, I said to Sapt, was the real danger.

"And there," I added, "you shall be. Doesn't that content you?"

But it did not. Dearly would he have liked to come with me had I not utterly refused to take him. One man might escape notice; to double the party more than doubled the risk; and when he ventured to hint once again that my life was too valuable, I, knowing the secret thought he clung to, sternly bade him be silent, assuring him that unless the king lived through the night I would not live through it either.

At twelve o'clock Sapt's command left the chateau of Tarlenheim and struck off to the right, riding by unfrequented roads and avoiding the town of Zenda. If all went well they would be in front of Zenda by about a quarter to two. Leaving their horses half a mile off, they were to steal up to the entrance and hold themselves in readiness for the opening of the door. If the door were not opened by two, they were to send Fritz von Tarlenheim round to the other side of the castle. I would meet him there if I were alive, and we would consult whether to storm the castle or not. If I were not there they were to return with all speed to Tarlenheim, rouse the marshal and march in force on Zenda. For if not there I should be dead, and I knew that the king would not be alive five minutes after I had ceased to breathe.

I must now leave Sapt and his friends, and relate how I myself proceeded on this eventful night. I went out on the good horse which had carried me, on the night of the coronation, back from the shooting lodge to Strelsau. I carried a revolver in the saddle and my sword. I was covered with a large cloak, and under this I wore a warm, tightfitting woollen jersey, a pair of knickerbockers, thick stockings, and light canvas shoes. I had rubbed myself thoroughly with oil, and I carried a large flask of whisky. The night was warm, but I might probably be immersed a long while, and it was necessary to take every precaution against cold, for cold not only saps a man's courage if he has to die but impairs his energy if others have to die, and, finally, gives him rheumatics, if it be God's will that he lives. Also I tied round my body a length of thin but stout cord, and I did not forget my ladder. I, starting after Sapt, took a shorter route, skirting the town to the left, and found myself in the outskirts of the forest at about half-past twelve. I tied my horse up in a thick clump of trees, leaving the revolver in its pocket in the saddle—it would be no use to me—and, ladder in hand, made my way to the edge of the moat. Here I unwound my rope from about my waist, bound it securely round the trunk of a tree on the bank, and let myself down. The castle clock struck a quarter to one as I felt the water under me and began to swim round the keep, pushing the ladder before me and hugging the castle wall. Thus voyaging, I came to my old friend "Jacob's ladder", and felt the ledge of masonry under me. I crouched down in the shadow of the great pipe—I tried to stir it, but it was quite immovable—and waited. I remembered that my predominant feeling was neither anxiety for the king nor longing for Flavia, but an intense desire to smoke, and this craving, of course, I could not gratify.

The drawbridge was still in its place. I saw its airy, light framework above me, some ten yards to my right, as I crouched with my back against the wall of the king's cell. I made out a window two yards my side of it and nearly on the same level. That, if Johann spoke true, must belong to the duke's apartments; and on the other side, in about the same relative position, must be Mme de Mauban's window. Women are careless, forgetful creatures. I prayed that she might not forget that she was to be the victim of a brutal attempt at two o'clock precisely. I was rather amused at the part I had assigned to my young friend Rupert Hentzau, but I owed him a stroke—for, even as I sat, my shoulder ached where he had, with an audacity that seemed half to hide his treachery, struck at me, in sight of all my friends, on the terrace at Tarlenheim.

Suddenly the duke's window grew bright. The shutters were not closed, and the interior became partially visible to me as I cautiously raised myself till I stood on tiptoe. Thus placed, my range of sight embraced a yard or more inside the window, while the radius of light did not reach me. The window was flung open and someone looked out. I marked Antoinette de Mauban's graceful figure, and though her face was in shadow, the fine outline of her head was revealed against the light behind. I longed to cry softly "Remember!" but I dared not—and happily, for a moment later a man came up and stood by her. He tried to put his arm round her waist, but with a swift motion she sprang away and leaned against the shutter, her profile towards me. I made out who the newcomer was: it was young Rupert. A low laugh from him made me sure, as he leaned forwards, stretching out his hand towards her.

"Gently, gently!" I murmured. "You're too soon, my boy!"

His head was close to hers. I suppose he whispered to her, for I saw her point to the moat, and I heard her say in slow and distinct tones: "I had rather throw myself out of this window!"

He came close up to the window and looked out.

"It looks cold," said he. "Come, Antoinette, are you serious?"

She made no answer, so far as I heard, and he, smiting his hand petulantly on the windowsill, went on in the voice of some spoilt child: "Hang Black Michael! Isn't the princess enough for him? Is he to have everything? What the devil do you see in Black Michael?"

"If I told him what you say—" she began.

"Well, tell him," said Rupert carelessly, and, catching her off her guard, he sprang forwards and kissed her, laughing, and crying, "There's something to tell him!"

If I had kept my revolver with me I should have been very sorely tempted. Being spared the temptation, I merely added this new score to his account.

"Though, faith," said Rupert, "it's little he cares. He's mad about the princess, you know. He talks of nothing but cutting the play-actor's throat."

Didn't he, indeed?

"And if I do it for him what do you think he's promised me?"

The unhappy woman raised her hands above her head, in prayer or in despair.

"But I detest waiting," said Rupert, and I saw that he was about to lay his hand on her again when there was a noise of a door in the room opening, and a harsh voice cried: "What are you doing here, sir?"

Rupert turned his back to the window, bowed low, and said in his loud, merry tones: "Apologizing for your absence, sir. Could I leave the lady alone?"

The newcomer must be Black Michael. I saw him directly, as he advanced towards the window. He caught young Rupert by the arm.

"The moat would hold more than the king!" said he, with a significant gesture.

"Does your Highness threaten me?" asked Rupert.

"A threat is more warning than most men get from me."

"Yet," observed Rupert, "Rudolf Rassendyll has been much threatened and yet lives!"

"Am I in fault because my servants bungle?" asked Michael scornfully.

"Your Highness has run no risk of bungling!" sneered Rupert.

It was telling the duke that he shirked danger as plain as ever I have heard a man told. Black Michael had self-control. I dare say he scowled—it was a great regret to me that I could not see their faces better—but his voice was even and calm as he answered: "Enough, enough! We mustn't quarrel, Rupert. Are Detchard and Bersonin at their posts?"

"They are, sir."

"I need you no more."

"Nay, I'm not oppressed with fatigue," said Rupert.

"Pray, sir, leave us," said Michael more impatiently. "In ten minutes the drawbridge will be drawn back, and I presume you have no wish to swim to your bed."

Rupert's figure disappeared. I heard the door open and shut again. Michael and Antoinette de Mauban were left together. To my chagrin, the duke laid his hand on the window and closed it. He stood talking to Antoinette for a moment or two. She shook her head, and he turned impatiently away. She left the window. The door sounded again, and Black Michael closed the shutters.

"De Gautet, De Gautet, man!" sounded from the drawbridge. "Unless you want a bath before your bed, come along!"

It was Rupert's voice, coming from the end of the drawbridge. A moment later he and De Gautet stepped out on the bridge. Rupert's arm was through De Gautet's, and in the middle of the bridge he detained his companion and leaned over. I dropped beside the shelter of "Jacob's ladder".

Then Master Rupert had a little sport. He took from De Gautet a bottle which he carried and put it to his lips.

"Hardly a drop!" he cried discontentedly, and flung it in the moat.

It fell, as I judged from the sound and the circles on the water, within a yard of the pipe. And Rupert, taking out his revolver, began to shoot at it. The first two shots missed the bottle but hit the pipe. The third shattered the bottle. I hoped that the young ruffian would be content, but he emptied the other barrels at the pipe, and one, skimming over the pipe, whistled through my hair as I crouched on the other side.

"'Ware bridge!" a voice cried, to my relief.

Rupert and De Gautet cried, "A moment!" and ran across. The bridge was drawn back, and all became still. The clock struck a quarter past one. I rose and stretched myself and yawned.

I think some ten minutes had passed when I heard a slight noise to my right. I peered over the pipe and saw a dark figure standing in the gateway that led to the bridge. It was a man. By the careless, graceful poise I guessed it to be Rupert again. He held a sword in his hand, and he stood motionless for a minute or two. Wild thoughts ran through me. On what mischief was the young fiend bent now? Then he laughed low to himself; then he turned his face to the wall, took a step in my direction, and to my surprise began to climb down the wall. In an instant I saw that there must be steps in the wall; it was plain. They were cut into or affixed to the wall at intervals of about eighteen inches. Rupert set his foot on the lower one. Then he placed his sword between his teeth, turned round and noiselessly let himself down into the water. Had it been a matter of my life only, I would have swum to meet him. Dearly would I have loved to fight it out with him then and there—with steel, on a fine night and none to come between us. But there was the king! I restrained myself, but I could not bridle my swift breathing, and I watched him with the intensest eagerness.

He swam leisurely and quietly across. There were more foot steps up on the other side, and he climbed them. When he set foot in the gateway, standing on the drawn-back bridge, he felt in his pocket and took something out. I heard him unlock the door. I could hear no noise of its closing behind him. He vanished from my sight.

Abandoning my ladder—I saw I did not need it now—I swam to the side of the bridge and climbed halfway up the steps. There I hung, with my sword in my hand, listening eagerly. The duke's room was shuttered and dark. There was a light in the window on the opposite side of the bridge. Not a sound broke the silence, till half-past one chimed from the great clock in the tower of the chateau.

There were other plots than mine afoot in the castle that night.

18

The Forcing of the Trap

The position wherein I stood does not appear very favourable to thought, yet for the next moment or two I thought profoundly. I had, I told myself, scored one point. Be Rupert Hentzau's errand what it might and the villainy he was engaged on what it would, I had scored one point. He was on the other side of the moat from the king, and it would be by no fault of mine if ever he set foot on the same side again. I had three left to deal with: two on guard and De Gautet in his bed. Ah, if I had the keys! I would have risked everything and attacked Detchard and Bersonin before their friends could join them. But I was powerless. I must wait till the coming of my friends enticed someone to cross the bridge—someone with the keys. And I waited, as it seemed, for half an hour, really for about five minutes, before the next act in the rapid drama began.

All was still on the other side. The duke's room remained inscrutable behind its shutters. The light burned steadily in Mme de Mauban's window. Then I heard the faintest, faintest sound; it came from behind the door which led to the drawbridge on the other side of the moat. It but just reached my ear, yet I could not be mistaken as to what it was. It was made by a key being turned very carefully and slowly. Who was turning it? And of what room was it the key? There leaped before my eyes the picture of young Rupert, with the key in one hand, his sword in the other, and an evil smile on his face. But I did not know what door it was, nor in which of his favourite pursuits young Rupert was spending the hours of that night.

I was soon to be enlightened, for the next moment—before my

friends could be near the chateau door—before Johann, the keeper, would have thought to nerve himself for his task—there was a sudden crash from the room with the lighted window. It sounded as though someone had flung down a lamp, and the window went dark and black. At the same instant a cry rang out, shrill in the night: "Help, help! Michael, help!" and was followed by a shriek of utter terror.

I was tingling in every nerve. I stood on the topmost step, clinging to the threshold of the gate with my right hand and holding my sword in my left. Suddenly I perceived that the gateway was broader than the bridge; there was a dark corner on the opposite side where a man could stand. I darted across and stood there. Thus placed, I commanded the path, and no man could pass between the chateau and the old castle till he had tried conclusions with me.

There was another shriek. Then a door was flung open and clanged against the wall, and I heard the handle of a door savagely twisted.

"Open the door! In God's name, what's the matter?" cried a voice—the voice of Black Michael himself.

He was answered by the very words I had written in my letter: "Help, Michael—Hentzau!"

A fierce oath rang out from the duke, and with a loud thud he threw himself against the door. At the same moment I heard a window above my head open, and a voice cried: "What's the matter?" and I heard a man's hasty footsteps. I grasped my sword. If De Gautet came my way the Six would be less by one more.

Then I heard the clash of crossed swords and a tramp of feet, and—I cannot tell the thing so quickly as it happened, for all seemed to come at once. There was an angry cry from madame's room, the cry of a wounded man; the window was flung open; young Rupert stood there, sword in hand. He turned his back, and I saw his body go forwards to the lunge.

"Ah, Johann, there's one for you! Come on, Michael!"

Johann was there, then—come to the rescue of the duke! How would he open the door for me? For I feared that Rupert had slain him.

"Help!" cried the duke's voice, faint and husky.

I heard a stir on the stairs above me, and I heard a stir down to my right, in the direction of the king's cell. But before anything happened on my side of the moat, I saw five or six men round young Rupert in the embrasure of madame's window. Three or four times he lunged with incomparable dash and dexterity. For an instant they fell back, leaving a ring round him. He leaped on the parapet of the window, laughing as he leaped and waving his sword in his hand. He was drunk with blood, and he laughed again wildly as he flung himself headlong into the moat.

What became of him then? I did not see, for as he leaped, De Gautet's lean face looked out through the door by me, and without a second's hesitation I struck at him with all the strength God had given me, and he fell dead in the doorway without a word or a groan. I dropped on my knees by him. Where were the keys? I found myself muttering: "The keys, man, the keys?" as though he had been yet alive and could listen; and when I could not find them I—God forgive me!—I believe I struck a dead man's face.

At last I had them. There were but three. Seizing the largest, I felt the lock of the door that led to the cell. I fitted in the key. It was right! The lock turned. I drew the door close behind me and locked it as noiselessly as I could, putting the key in my pocket.

I found myself at the top of a flight of steep stone stairs. An oil lamp burned dimly in the bracket. I took it down and held it in my hand; and I stood and listened.

"What in the devil can it be?" I heard a voice say.

It came from behind a door that faced me at the bottom of the stairs.

And another answered: "Shall we kill him?"

I strained to hear the answer and could have sobbed with relief when Detchard's voice came grating and cold: "Wait a bit. There'll be trouble if we strike too soon."

There was a moment's silence. Then I heard the bolt of the door cautiously drawn back. Instantly I put out the light I held, replacing the lamp in the bracket.

"It's dark—the lamp's out. Have you a light?" said the other voice—Bersonin's.

No doubt they had a light, but they should not use it. It was come to the crisis now, and I rushed down the steps and flung myself against the door. Bersonin had unbolted it, and it gave way before me. The Belgian stood there, sword in hand, and Detchard was sitting on a couch at the side of the room. In astonishment at seeing me, Bersonin recoiled; Detchard jumped to his sword. I rushed madly at the Belgian. He gave way before me, and I drove him up against the wall. He was no swordsman, though he fought bravely, and in a moment he lay on the floor before me. I turned—Detchard was not there. Faithful to his orders, he had not risked a fight with me but had rushed straight to the door of the king's room, opened it and slammed it behind him. Even now he was at his work inside.

And surely he would have killed the king, and perhaps me also, had it not been for one devoted man who gave his life for the king. For when I forced the door the sight I saw was this: The king stood in the corner of the room; broken by his sickness, he could do nothing; his fettered hands moved uselessly up and down, and he was laughing horribly in half-mad delirium. Detchard and the doctor were together in the middle of the room; and the doctor had flung himself on the murderer, pinning his hands to his sides for an instant. Then Detchard wrenched himself free from the feeble grip, and as I entered drove his sword through the hapless man.

Then he turned on me, crying: "At last!"

We were sword to sword. By blessed chance neither he nor Bersonin had been wearing their revolvers. I found them afterwards, ready loaded, on the mantelpiece of the outer room; it was hard by the door, ready to their hands, but my sudden rush in had cut off access to them. Yes, we were man to man, and we began to fight, silently, sternly, and hard. Yet I remember little of it, save that the man was my match with the sword—nay, and more, for he knew more tricks than I; and that he forced me back against the bars that guarded the entrance to "Jacob's ladder". And I saw a smile on his face, and he wounded me in the left arm.

No glory do I take for that contest. I believe that the man would have mastered me and slain me, and then done his butcher's work, for he was the most skilful swordsman I have ever met, but even as he pressed me hard, the half-mad, wasted, wan creature in the corner leaped high in lunatic mirth, shrieking: "It's Cousin Rudolf! Cousin Rudolf! I'll help you, Cousin Rudolf!" and catching up a chair in his hands (he could but just lift it from the ground and hold it uselessly before him), he came towards us. Hope came to me.

"Come on!" I cried. "Come on! Drive it against his legs."

Detchard replied with a savage thrust. He all but had me.

"Come on! Come on, man!" I cried. "Come and share the fun!"

And the king laughed gleefully and came on, pushing his chair before him.

With an oath Detchard skipped back, and before I knew what he was doing had turned his sword against the king. He made one fierce cut at the king, and the king, with a piteous cry, dropped where he stood. The stout ruffian turned to face me again. But his own hand had prepared his destruction, for in turning he trod in the pool of blood that flowed from the dead physician. He slipped; he fell. Like a dart I was upon him. I caught him by the throat, and before he could recover himself I drove my blade through his neck, and with a stifled curse he fell across the body of his victim.

Was the king dead? It was my first thought. I rushed to where he lay. Aye, it seemed as if he were dead, for he had a great gash across the forehead, and he lay still in a huddled mass on the floor. I dropped on my knees beside him and leaned my ear down to hear if he breathed. But before I could, there was a loud rattle from the outside. I knew the sound; the drawbridge was being pushed out. A moment later it rang home against the wall on my side of the moat. I should be caught in a trap and the king with me, if he yet lived. He must take his chance, to live or to die. I took my sword and passed into the outer room. Who were pushing the drawbridge out—my men? If so, all was well. My eye fell on the revolvers, and I seized one; and paused to listen in the doorway of the outer room. To listen, say I? Yes, and to get my breath; and I tore my shirt and twisted a strip of it round my bleeding arm; and stood listening again. I would have given the world to hear Sapt's voice. For I was faint, spent, and weary. And that wildcat Rupert Hentzau was yet at large in the castle. Yet, because I could better defend the narrow door at the top of the stairs than the wider entrance to the room, I dragged myself up the steps, and stood behind it, listening.

What was the sound? Again a strange one for the place and the time. An easy, scornful, merry laugh—the laugh of young Rupert Hentzau! I could scarcely believe that a sane man would laugh. Yet the laugh told me that my men had not come, for they must have shot Rupert ere now if they had come. And the clock struck half-past two! My God! The door had not been opened! They had gone to the bank! They had not found me! They had gone by now back to Tarlenheim with the news of the king's death—and mine. Well, it would be true before they got there. Was not Rupert laughing with triumph?

For a moment I sank, unnerved, against the door. Then I started up alert again, for Rupert cried scornfully: "Well, the bridge is there! Come over it! And in God's name, let's see Black Michael keep back you curs! Michael, come and fight for her!"

If it were a three-cornered fight I might yet bear my part. I turned the key in the door and looked out.

19

Face to Face in the Forest

For a moment I could see nothing, for the glare of lanterns and torches caught me full in the eyes from the other side of the bridge. But soon the scene grew clear, and it was a strange scene. The bridge was in its place. At the far end of it stood a group of the duke's servants; two or three carried the lights which had dazzled me, three or four held pikes in rest. They were huddled together; their weapons were protruded before them; their faces were pale and agitated. To put it plainly, they looked in as arrant a fright as I have seen men look, and they gazed apprehensively at a man who stood in the middle of the bridge, sword in hand. Rupert Hentzau was in his trousers and shirt; the white linen was stained with blood; but his easy, buoyant pose told me that he was himself either not touched at all or merely scratched. There he stood, holding the bridge against them and daring them to come on; or, rather, bidding them and Black Michael to him; and they, having no firearms, cowered before the desperate man and dared not attack him. They whispered to one another, and in the backmost rank I saw my friend Johann, leaning against the portal of the door and staunching with a handkerchief the blood which flowed from a wound in his cheek.

By marvellous chance I was master. The cravens would oppose me no more than they dared attack Rupert. I had but to raise my revolver, and I sent him to his account with his sins on his head. He did not so much as know that I was there. I did nothing—why, I hardly know to this day. I had killed one man stealthily that night, and another by luck rather than skill—perhaps it was that. Again, villain as the man was, I did not relish being one of a crowd against him—perhaps it was that. But stronger than either of these restraining feelings came a curiosity and a fascination which held me spellbound, watching for the outcome of the scene.

"Michael, you dog! Michael! If you can stand, come on!" cried Rupert, and he advanced a step, the group shrinking back a little before him. "Michael, you bastard! Come on!"

The answer to his taunts came in the wild cry of a woman: "He's dead! My God, he's dead!"

"Dead!" shouted Rupert. "I struck better than I knew!" and he laughed triumphantly. Then he went on: "Down with your weapons there! I'm your master now! Down with them, I say!"

I believe they would have obeyed, but as he spoke came new things. First, there arose a distant sound, as of shouts and knockings from the other side of the chateau. My heart leaped. It must be my men, come by a happy disobedience to seek me. The noise continued, but none of the rest seemed to heed it. Their attention was chained by what now happened before their eyes. The group of servants parted, and a woman staggered on to the bridge. Antoinette de Mauban was in a loose white robe, her dark hair streamed over her shoulders, her face was ghastly pale, and her eyes gleamed wildly in the light of the torches. In her shaking hand she held a revolver, and as she tottered forwards she fired it at Rupert Hentzau. The ball missed him and struck the woodwork over my head.

"Faith, madame," laughed Rupert, "had your eyes been no more deadly than your shooting I had not been in this scrape— nor Black Michael in hell—tonight!"

She took no notice of his words. With a wonderful effort she calmed herself till she stood still and rigid. Then very slowly and deliberately she began to raise her arm again, taking most careful aim.

He would be mad to risk it. He must rush on her, chancing the bullet, or retreat towards me. I covered him with my weapon.

He did neither. Before she had got her aim he bowed in his most gracious fashion, cried, "I can't kill where I've kissed," and before she or I could stop him laid his hand on the parapet of the bridge and lightly leaped into the moat.

At the very moment I heard a rush of feet and a voice I knew—Sapt's—cry: "God! It's the duke—dead!" Then I knew that the king needed me no more, and, throwing down my revolver, I sprang out on the bridge. There was a cry of wild wonder, "The king!" and then I, like Rupert Hentzau, sword in hand, vaulted over the parapet, intent on finishing my quarrel with him where I saw his curly head fifteen yards off in the water of the moat.

He swam swiftly and easily. I was weary and half crippled with my wounded arm. I could not gain on him. For a time I made no sound, but as we rounded the corner of the old keep I cried: "Stop, Rupert, stop!"

I saw him look over his shoulder, but he swam on. He was under the bank now, searching, as I guessed, for a spot that he could climb. I knew there to be none—but there was my rope, which would still be hanging where I had left it. He would come to where it was before I could. Perhaps he would miss it—perhaps he would find it; and if he drew it up after him he would get a good start on me. I put forth all my remaining strength and pressed on. At last I began to gain on him; for he, occupied with his search, unconsciously slackened his pace.

Ah, he had found it! A low shout of triumph came from him. He laid hold of it and began to haul himself up. I was near enough to hear him mutter: "How the devil comes this here?" I was at the rope, and he, hanging in midair, saw me, but I could not reach him.

"Hullo! Who's there?" he cried in startled tones.

For a moment I believe he took me for the king—I dare say I was pale enough to lend colour to the thought, but an instant later he cried: "Why, it's the play-actor! How came you here, man?"

And so saying he gained the bank.

I laid hold of the rope, but I paused. He stood on the bank, sword in hand, and he could cut my head open or spit me through the heart as I came up. I let go the rope.

"Never mind," said I, "but as I am here I think I'll stay."

He smiled down on me.

"These women are the deuce—" he began, when suddenly the great bell of the castle began to ring furiously, and a loud shout reached us from the moat.

Rupert smiled again and waved his hand to me.

"I should like a turn with you, but it's a little too hot!" said he, and he disappeared from above me.

In an instant, without thinking of danger, I laid my hand to the rope. I was up. I saw him thirty yards off, running like a deer towards the shelter of the forest. For once Rupert Hentzau had chosen discretion for his part. I laid my feet to the ground and rushed after him, calling to him to stand. He would not. Unwounded and vigorous, he gained on me at every step; but, forgetting everything in the world except him and my thirst for his blood, I pressed on, and soon the deep shades of the forest of Zenda engulfed us both, pursued and pursuer.

It was three o'clock now, and day was dawning. I was on a long, straight grass avenue, and a hundred yards ahead ran young Rupert, his curls waving in the fresh breeze. I was weary and panting; he looked over his shoulder and waved his hand again to me. He was mocking me, for he saw he had the pace of me. I was forced to pause for breath. A moment later Rupert turned sharply to the right and was lost from my sight.

I thought all was over, and in deep vexation sank on the ground. But I was up again directly, for a scream rang through the forest—a woman's scream. Putting forth the last of my strength, I ran on to the place where he had turned out of my sight, and turning also, I saw him again. But alas! I could not touch him. He was in the act of lifting a girl down from her horse; doubtless it was her scream that I heard. She looked like a small farmer's or a peasant's daughter, and she carried a basket on her arm. Probably she was on her way to the early market at Zenda. Her horse was a stout, well-shaped animal. Master Rupert lifted her down amid her shrieks—the sight of him frightened her; but he treated her gently, laughed, kissed her, and gave her money. Then he jumped on the horse, sitting sideways like a woman; and then he waited for me. I, on my part, waited for him.

Presently he rode towards me, keeping his distance however. He lifted up his hand, saying: "What did you in the castle?"

"I killed three of your friends," said I.

"What! You got to the cells?"

"Yes."

"And the king?"

"He was hurt by Detchard before I killed Detchard, but I pray that he lives."

"You fool!" said Rupert pleasantly.

"One thing more I did."

"And what's that?"

"I spared your life. I was behind you on the bridge, with a revolver in my hand."

"No? Faith, I was between two fires!"

"Get off your horse," I cried, "and fight like a man."

"Before a lady!" said he, pointing to the girl. "Fie, your Majesty!"

Then in my rage, hardly knowing what I did, I rushed at him. For a moment he seemed to waver, then he reined his horse in and stood waiting for me. On I went in my folly. I seized the bridle and I struck at him. He parried and thrust at me. I fell back a pace and rushed in at him again; and this time I reached his face and laid his cheek open, and darted back before he could strike me. He seemed almost dazed at the fierceness of my attack; otherwise I think he must have killed me. I sank on my knee, panting, expecting him to ride at me. And so he would have done, and then and there, I doubt not, one or both of us would have died; but at the moment there came a shout from behind us, and, looking round, I saw just at the turn of the avenue a man on a horse. He was riding hard, and he carried a revolver in his hands. It was Fritz von Tarlenheim, my faithful friend. Rupert saw him, and knew that the game was up. He checked his rush at me and flung his leg over the saddle, but yet for just a moment he waited. Leaning forwards, he tossed his hair off his forehead and smiled, and said: "Au revoir, Rudolf Rassendyll!"

Then, with his cheek streaming blood, but his lips laughing and his body swaying with ease and grace, he bowed to me; and he bowed to the farm girl, who had drawn near in trembling fascination; and he waved his hand to Fritz, who was just within range and let fly a shot at him. The ball came nigh doing its work, for it struck the sword he held, and he dropped the sword with an oath, wringing his fingers, and clapped his heels hard in his horse's belly, and rode away at a gallop.

And I watched him go down the long avenue, riding as though he rode for his pleasure and singing as he went, for all there was that gash in his cheek.

Once again he turned to wave his hand, and then the gloom of the thickets swallowed him and he was lost from our sight. Thus he vanished—reckless and wary, graceful and graceless, handsome, debonair, vile, and unconquered. And I flung my sword passionately on the ground and cried to Fritz to ride after him. But Fritz stopped his horse, and leaped down and ran to me, and knelt, putting his arm about me. And indeed it was time, for the wound that Detchard had given me was broken forth afresh, and my blood was staining the ground.

"Then give me the horse!" I cried, staggering to my feet and throwing his arms off me. And the strength of my rage carried me so far as to where the horse stood, and then I fell prone beside it. And Fritz knelt by me again.

"Fritz!" I said.

"Aye, friend—dear friend!" said he, tender as a woman.

"Is the king alive?"

He took his handkerchief and wiped my lips, and bent and kissed me on the forehead.

"Thanks to the most gallant gentleman that lives," said he softly, "the king is alive!"

The little farm girl stood by us, weeping for fright and wide-eyed for wonder, for she had seen me at Zenda, and was not I, pallid, dripping, foul, and bloody as I was—yet was not I the king?

And when I heard that the king was alive I strove to cry "Hurrah!" But I could not speak, and I laid my head back in Fritz's arms and closed my eyes, and I groaned; and then, lest Fritz should do me wrong in his thoughts, I opened my eyes and tried to say "Hurrah!" again. But I could not. And being very tired, and now very cold, I huddled myself close up to Fritz to get the warmth of him, and shut my eyes again and went to sleep.

20

The Prisoner and the King

In order to a full understanding of what had occurred in the castle
of Zenda it is necessary to supplement my account of what I myself saw and did on that night by relating briefly what I afterwards
learned from Fritz and from Mme de Mauban. The story told by
the latter explained clearly how it happened that the cry which I
had arranged as a stratagem and a sham had come, in dreadful reality, before its time, and had thus, as it seemed at the moment,
ruined our hopes, while in the end it had favoured them. The unhappy woman, fired, I believe, by a genuine attachment to the
Duke of Strelsau no less than by the dazzling prospects which a
dominion over him opened before her eyes, had followed him at
his request from Paris to Ruritania. He was a man of strong passions but of stronger will, and his cool head ruled both. He was
content to take all and give nothing. When she arrived she was
not long in finding that she had a rival in the Princess Flavia. Ren-
dered desperate, she stood at nothing which might give or keep
for her her power over the duke. As I say, he took and gave not.
Simultaneously Antoinette found herself entangled in his audacious schemes. Unwilling to abandon him, bound to him by the
chains of shame and hope, she yet would not be a decoy, nor at
his bidding lure me to death. Hence the letters of warning she had
written. Whether the lines she sent to Flavia were inspired by
good or bad feeling, by jealousy or by pity, I do not know; but
here also she served us well. When the duke went to Zenda she
accompanied him; and here for the first time she learned the full
measure of his cruelty and was touched with compassion for

140

the unfortunate king. From this time she was with us; yet, from what she told me, I know that she still (as women will) loved Michael and trusted to gain his life, if not his pardon, from the king as the reward for her assistance. His triumph she did not desire, for she loathed his crime and loathed yet more fiercely what would be the prize of it—his marriage with his cousin, Princess Flavia.

At Zenda new forces came into play—the lust and daring of young Rupert. He was caught by her beauty, perhaps; perhaps it was enough for him that she belonged to another man and that she hated him. For many days there had been quarrels and ill will between him and the duke, and the scene which I had witnessed in the duke's room was but one of many. Rupert's proposals to me, of which she had of course been ignorant, in no way surprised her when I related them. She had herself warned Michael against Rupert, even when she was calling on me to deliver her from both of them. On this night, then, Rupert had determined to have his will. When she had gone to her room he, having furnished himself with a key to it, had made his entrance. Her cries had brought the duke, and there in the dark room while she screamed, the men had fought; and Rupert, having wounded his master with a mortal blow, had, on the servants rushing in, escaped through the window as I have described. The duke's blood, spurting out, had stained his opponent's shirt; but Rupert, not knowing that he had dealt Michael his death, was eager to finish the encounter. How he meant to deal with the other three of the band I know not. I dare say he did not think, for the killing of Michael was not premeditated. Antoinette, left alone with the duke, had tried to staunch his wound, and thus was she busied till he died; and then, hearing Rupert's taunts, she had come forth to avenge him. Me she had not seen, nor did she till I darted out of my ambush and leaped after Rupert into the moat.

The same moment found my friends on the scene. They had reached the chateau in due time, and waited ready by the door. But Johann, swept with the rest to the rescue of the duke, did not open it; nay, he took a part against Rupert, putting himself forward more bravely than any in his anxiety to avert suspicion; and he had received a wound, in the embrasure of the window. Till nearly half-past two Sapt waited; then, following my orders, he had sent Fritz to search the banks of the moat. I was not there. Hastening back, Fritz told Sapt; and Sapt was for following orders still and riding at full speed back to Tarlenheim; while Fritz would not hear of abandoning me, let me have ordered what I would. On this they disputed some few minutes, then Sapt, persuaded by Fritz, detached a party under Bernenstein to gallop back to Tarlenheim and bring up the marshal, while the rest fell to on the great door of the chateau. For near fifteen minutes it resisted them; then, just as Antoinette de Mauban fired at Rupert Hentzau on the bridge, they broke in, eight of them in all; and the first door they came to was the door of Michael's room; and Michael lay dead across the threshold, with a sword thrust through his breast. Sapt cried out at his death, as I had heard, and they rushed on the servants; but these, in fear, dropped their weapons, and Antoinette flung herself weeping at Sapt's feet. And all she cried was that I had been at the end of the bridge and had leaped off. "What of the prisoner?" asked Sapt, but she shook her head. Then Sapt and Fritz, with the gentlemen behind them, crossed the bridge, slowly, warily, and without noise; and Fritz stumbled over the body of De Gautet in the way of the door. They felt him and found him dead.

Then they consulted, listening eagerly for any sound from the cells below; but there came none, and they were greatly afraid that the king's guards had killed him, and having pushed his body through the great pipe, had escaped the same way themselves. Yet, because I had been seen here, they had still some hope (thus indeed Fritz, in his friendship, told me); and going back to Michael's body, pushing aside Antoinette, who prayed by it, they found a key to the door which I had locked, and opened the door. The staircase was dark, and they would not use the torch at first, lest they should be the more exposed to fire. But soon Fritz cried: "The door down there is open! See, there is light!" So they went on boldly and found none to oppose them. And when they came to the outer room and saw the Belgian, Bersonin, lying dead, they thanked God, Sapt saying: "Aye, he has been here." Then rushing into the king's cell, they found Detchard lying dead across the dead physician, and the king on his back with his chair by him. And Fritz cried: "He's dead!" and Sapt drove all out of the room except Fritz and knelt down by the king; and, having learned more of wounds and the signs of death than I, he soon knew that the king was not dead, nor, if properly attended, would die. And they covered his face and carried him to Duke Michael's room, and laid him there; and Antoinette rose from praying by the body of the duke and went to bathe the king's head and dress his wounds, till a doctor came. And Sapt, seeing I had been there and having heard Antoinette's story, sent Fritz to search the moat and then the forest. He dared send no one else. And Fritz found my horse and feared the worst. Then, as I have told, he found me, guided by the shout with which I had called on Rupert to stop and face me. And I think a man has never been more glad to find his own brother alive than was Fritz to come on me; so that, in love and anxiety for me, he thought nothing of a thing so great as would have been the death of Rupert Hentzau. Yet had Fritz killed him I should have grudged it.

The enterprise of the king's rescue being thus prosperously concluded, it lay on Colonel Sapt to secure secrecy as to the king ever having been in need of rescue. Antoinette de Mauban and Johann, the keeper (who, indeed, was too much hurt to be wagging his tongue just now) were sworn to reveal nothing; and Fritz went forth to find—not the king, but the unnamed friend of the king, who had lain in Zenda and flashed for a moment before the dazed eyes of Duke Michael's servants on the drawbridge. The metamorphosis had happened, and the king, wounded almost to death by the attacks of the jailers who guarded his friend, had at last overcome them and rested now, wounded but alive, in Black Michael's own room in the castle. There he had been carried, his face covered with a cloak, from the cell; and thence orders issued that if his friend were found he should be brought directly and privately to the king, and that meanwhile messengers should ride at full speed to Tarlenheim to tell Marshal Strakencz to assure the princess of the king's safety and to come himself with all speed to greet the king. The princess was enjoined to remain at Tarlenheim and there await her cousin's coming or his further injunctions. Thus the king would come to his own again, having wrought brave deeds and escaped, almost by a miracle, the treacherous assault of his unnatural brother.

This ingenious arrangement of my long-headed old friend prospered in every way, save where it encountered a force that often defeats the most cunning schemes. I mean nothing else than the pleasure of a woman. For let her cousin and sovereign send what command he chose (or Colonel Sapt chose for him), and let Marshal Strakencz insist as he would, the Princess Flavia was in no way minded to rest at Tarlenheim while her lover lay wounded at Zenda; and when the marshal, with a small suite, rode forth from Tarlenheim on the way to Zenda the princess's carriage followed immediately behind, and in this order they passed through the town, where the report was already rife that the king, going the night before to remonstrate with his brother, in all friendliness, for that he held one of the king's friends in confinement in the castle had been most traitorously set upon; that there had been a desperate conflict; that the duke was slain with several of his gentlemen; and that the king, wounded as he was, had seized and held the castle of Zenda. All of which talk made, as may be supposed, a mighty excitement; and the wires were set in motion, and the tidings came to Strelsau only just after orders had been sent thither to parade the troops and overawe the dissatisfied quarters of the town with a display of force.

Thus the Princess Flavia came to Zenda. And as she drove up the hill, with the marshal riding by the wheel and still imploring her to return in obedience to the king's orders, Fritz von Tarlenheim, with the prisoner of Zenda, came to the edge of the forest. I had revived from my swoon and walked, resting on Fritz's arm, and looking out from the cover of the trees, I saw the princess. Suddenly understanding from a glance at my companion's face that we must not meet her, I sank on my knees behind a clump of bushes. But there was one whom we had forgotten but who followed us and was not disposed to let slip the chance of earning a smile and maybe a crown or two; and while we lay hidden the little farm girl came by us and ran to the princess, curtseying and crying: "Madame, the king is here—in the bushes! May I guide you to him, madame?"

"Nonsense, child!" said old Strakencz. "The king lies wounded in the castle."

"Yes, sir, he's wounded, I know; but he's there—with Count Fritz—and not at the castle," she persisted.

"Is he in two places or are there two kings? " asked Flavia, bewildered. "And how should he be here?"

"He pursued a gentleman, madame, and they fought till Count Fritz came; and the other gentleman took my father's horse from me and rode away; but the king is here with Count Fritz. Why, madame, is there another man in Ruritania like the king?"

"No, my child," said Flavia softly (I was told it afterwards), and she smiled and gave the girl money. "I will go and see this gentleman," and she rose to alight from the carriage.

But at this moment Sapt came riding from the castle and, seeing the princess, made the best of a bad job and cried to her that the king was well tended and in no danger.

"In the castle?" she asked.

"Where else, madame?" said he, bowing.

"But this girl says he is yonder—with Count Fritz."

Sapt turned his eyes on the child with an incredulous smile.

"Every fine gentleman is a king to such," said he.

"Why, he's as like the king as one pea to another, madame!" cried the girl, a little shaken, but still obstinate.

Sapt started round. The old marshal's face asked unspoken questions. Flavia's glance was no less eloquent. Suspicion spreads quick.

"I'll ride myself and see this man," said Sapt hastily.

"Nay, I'll come myself," said the princess.

"Then come alone," he whispered.

And she, obedient to the strange hinting in his face, prayed the marshal and the rest to wait; and she and Sapt came on foot towards where he lay, Sapt waving to the farm girl to keep at a distance. And when I saw them coming I sat in a sad heap on the ground and buried my face in my hands. I could not look at her. Fritz knelt by me, laying his hand on my shoulder.

"Speak low, whatever you say," I heard Sapt whisper as they came up, and the next thing I heard was a low cry—half of joy, half of fear—from the princess:

"It is he! Are you hurt?"

And she fell on the ground by me and gently pulled my hands away, but I kept my eyes to the ground.

"It is the king!" she said. "Pray, Colonel Sapt, tell me where lay the wit of the joke you played on me?"

We answered none of us. We three were silent before her. Regardless of them, she threw her arms round my neck and kissed me. Then Sapt spoke in a low, hoarse whisper: "It is not the king. Don't kiss him; he's not the king."

She drew back for a moment, then, with an arm still round my neck, she asked in superb indignation: "Do I not know my love? Rudolf, my love!"

"It is not the king," said old Sapt again, and a sudden sob broke from tenderhearted Fritz.

It was the sob that told her no comedy was afoot.

"He is the king!" she cried. "It is the king's face—the king's ring—my ring! It is my love!"

"Your love, madame," said old Sapt, "but not the king. The king is there in the castle. This gentleman—"

"Look at me, Rudolf! Look at me!" she cried, taking my face between her hands. "Why do you let them torment me? Tell me what it means!"

Then I spoke, gazing into her eyes.

"God forgive me, madame!" I said. "I am not the king!"

I felt her hands clutch my cheeks. She gazed at me as never man's face was scanned yet. And I, silent again, saw wonder born, and doubt grow, and terror spring to life as she looked. And very gradually the grasp of her hands slackened. She turned to Sapt, to Fritz, and back to me; then suddenly she reeled forwards and fell in my arms; and with a great cry of pain I gathered her to me and kissed her lips. Sapt laid his hand on my arm. I looked up in his face. And I laid her softly on the ground and stood up, looking on her, cursing Heaven that young Rupert's sword had spared me for this sharper pang.

21

If Love were All!

It was night, and I was in the cell wherein the king had lain in the castle of Zenda. The great pipe that Rupert of Hentzau had nicknamed "Jacob's ladder" was gone, and the lights in the room across the moat twinkled in the darkness. All was still; the din and clash of strife were gone. I had spent the day hidden in the forest from the time when Fritz had led me off, leaving Sapt with the princess. Under cover of dusk, muffled up, I had been brought to the castle and lodged where I now lay. Though three men had died there—two of them by my hand—I was not troubled by ghosts. I had thrown myself on a pallet by the window and was looking out on the black water; Johann, the keeper, still pale from his wound but not much hurt besides, had brought me supper. He told me that the king was doing well, that he had seen the princess; that she and he, Sapt and Fritz had been long together. Marshal Strakencz was gone to Strelsau; Black Michael lay in his coffin, and Antoinette de Mauban watched by him. Had I not heard from the chapel priests singing mass for him?

Outside there were strange rumours afloat. Some said that the prisoner of Zenda was dead; some, that he had vanished yet alive; some, that he was a friend who had served the king well in some adventure in England; others, that he had discovered the duke's plots and had therefore been kidnapped by him. One or two shrewd fellows shook their heads and said only that they would say nothing, but they had suspicions that more was to be known than was known if Colonel Sapt would tell all he knew.

Thus Johann chattered till I sent him away and lay there alone, thinking, not of the future, but—as a man is wont to do when stirring things have happened to him—rehearsing the events of the past weeks and wondering how strangely they had fallen out. And above me in the stillness of the night I heard the standards flapping against their poles, for Black Michael's banner hung there half-mast high, and above it the royal flag of Ruritania, floating for one night more over my head. Habit grows so quick that only by an effort did I recollect that it floated no longer for me.

Presently Fritz von Tarlenheim came into the room. I was standing then by the window; the glass was opened, and I was idly fingering the cement which clung to the masonry where "Jacob's ladder" had been. He told me briefly that the king wanted me, and together we crossed the drawbridge and entered the room that had been Black Michael's.

The king was lying there in bed; our doctor from Tarlenheim was in attendance on him and whispered to me that my visit must be brief. The king held out his hand and shook mine. Fritz and the doctor withdrew to the window.

I took the king's ring from my finger and placed it on his.

"I have tried not to dishonour it, sire," said I.

"I can't talk much to you," he said in a weak voice. "I have had a great fight with Sapt and the marshal—for we have told the marshal everything. I wanted to take you to Strelsau and keep you with me, and tell everyone of what you had done; and you would have been my best and nearest friend, Cousin Rudolf. But they tell me I must not and that the secret must be kept—if kept it can be."

"They are right, sire. Let me go. My work here is done."

"Yes, it is done, as no man but you could have done it. When they see me again I shall have my beard on; I shall—yes, faith, I shall be wasted with sickness. They will not wonder that the king looks changed in face. Cousin, I shall try to let them find him changed in nothing else. You have shown me how to play the king."

"Sire," said I, "I can take no praise from you. It is by the narrowest grace of God that I was not a worse traitor than your brother."

He turned inquiring eyes on me, but a sick man shrinks from puzzles, and he had no strength to question me. His glance fell on Flavia's ring, which I wore. I thought he would question me about it, but after fingering it idly he let his head fall on his pillow.

"I don't know when I shall see you again," he said faintly, almost listlessly.

"If I can ever serve you again, sire," I answered.

His eyelids closed. Fritz came with the doctor. I kissed the king's hand, and let Fritz lead me away. I have never seen the king since.

Outside, Fritz turned, not to the right, back towards the drawbridge, but to the left, and, without speaking, led me upstairs, through a handsome corridor in the chateau.

"Where are we going?" I asked.

Looking away from me, Fritz answered: "She has sent for you. When it is over come back to the bridge. I'll wait for you there."

"What does she want?" said I, breathing quickly.

He shook his head.

"Does she know everything?"

"Yes, everything."

He opened a door, and gently pushing me in, closed it behind me. I found myself in a drawing room, small and richly furnished. At first I thought that I was alone, for the light that came from a pair of shaded candles on the mantelpiece was very dim. But presently I discerned a woman's figure standing by the window. I knew it was the princess, and I walked up to her, fell on one knee, and carried the hand that hung by her side to my lips. She neither moved nor spoke. I rose to my feet, and, piercing the gloom with my eager eyes, saw her pale face and the gleam of her hair, and before I knew I spoke softly: "Flavia!"

She trembled a little, and looked round. Then she darted to me, taking hold of me.

"Don't stand, don't stand! No, you mustn't! You're hurt! Sit down—here, here!"

She made me sit on a sofa and put her hand on my forehead.

"How hot your head is!" she said, sinking on her knees by me.

Then she laid her head against me, and I heard her murmur: "My darling, how hot your head is!"

Somehow love gives even to a dull man the knowledge of his lover's heart. I had come to humble myself and pray pardon for my presumption, but what I said now was: "I love you with all my heart and soul!"

For what troubled and shamed her? Not her love for me, but the fear that I had counterfeited the lover as I had acted the king and taken her kisses with a smothered smile.

"With all my life and heart!" said I, as she clung to me. "Always, from the first moment I saw you in the cathedral! There has been but one woman in the world to me—and there will be no other. But God forgive me the wrong I've done you!"

"They made you do it!" she said quickly, and she added, raising her head and looking in my eyes: "It might have made no difference if I'd known it. It was always you, never the king!" and she raised herself and kissed me.

"I meant to tell you," said I. "I was going to on the night of the ball in Strelsau, when Sapt interrupted me. After that I couldn't— I couldn't risk losing you before—before—I must! My darling, for you I nearly left the king to die!"

"I know, I know! What are we to do now, Rudolf?"

I put my arm round her and held her up while I said: "I am going away tonight."

"Ah, no, no!" she cried. "Not tonight!"

"I must go tonight, before more people have seen me. And how would you have me stay, sweetheart, except—"

"If I could come with you!" she whispered very low.

"My God!" said I roughly, "don't talk about that!" and I thrust her a little back from me.

"Why not? I love you. You are as good a gentleman as the king!"

Then I was false to all that I should have held by. For I caught her in my arms and prayed her, in words that I will not write, to come with me, daring all Ruritania to take her from me. And for a while she listened, with wondering, dazzled eyes. But as her eyes looked on me I grew ashamed, and my voice died away in broken murmurs and stammerings, and at last I was silent.

She drew herself away from me and stood against the wall, while I sat on the edge of the sofa, trembling in every limb, knowing what I had done—loathing it, obstinate not to undo it. So we rested a long time.

"I am mad!" I said sullenly.

"I love your madness, dear," she answered.

Her face was away from me, but I caught the sparkle of a tear on her cheek. I clutched the sofa with my hand and held myself there.

"Is love the only thing?" she asked, in low, sweet tones that seemed to bring a calm even to my wrung heart. "If love were the only thing I could follow you—in rags, if need be—to the world's end, for you hold my heart in the hollow of your hand! But is love the only thing?"

I made her no answer. It gives me shame now to think that I would not help her.

She came near me and laid her hand on my shoulder. I put my hand up and held hers.

"I know people write and talk as if it were. Perhaps, for some, Fate lets it be. Ah, if I were one of them! But if love had been the only thing you would have let the king die in his cell."

I kissed her hand.

"Honour binds a woman too, Rudolf. My honour lies in being true to my country and my House. I don't know why God has let me love you, but I know that I must stay!"

Still I said nothing, and she, pausing a while, then went on: "Your ring will always be on my finger, your heart in my heart, the touch of your lips on mine. But you must go and I must stay. Perhaps I must do what it kills me to think of doing."

I knew what she meant, and a shiver ran through me. But I could not utterly fail beside her. I rose and took her hand.

"Do what you will or what you must," I said. "I think God shows his purposes to such as you. My part is lighter, for your ring shall be on my finger and your heart in mine, and no touch save of your lips will ever be on mine. So, may God comfort you, my darling!"

There struck on our ears the sound of singing. The priests in the chapel were singing masses for the souls of those who lay dead. They seemed to chant a requiem over our buried joy, to pray forgiveness for our love that would not die. The soft, sweet, pitiful music rose and fell as we stood opposite one another, her hands in mine.

"My queen and my beauty!" said I.

"My lover and true knight!" she said. "Perhaps we shall never see one another again. Kiss me, my dear, and go!"

I kissed her as she bade me, but at the last she clung to me, whispering nothing but my name, and that over and over again—and again—and again; and then I left her.

Rapidly I walked down to the bridge. Sapt and Fritz were waiting for me. Under their directions I changed my dress, and muffling my face, as I had done more than once before, I mounted with them at the door of the castle, and we three rode through the night and on to the breaking of day, and found ourselves at a little roadside station just over the border of Ruritania. The train was not quite due, and I walked with them in a meadow by a little brook while we waited for it. They promised to send me all news; they overwhelmed me with kindness—even old Sapt was touched to gentleness, while Fritz was half unmanned. I listened in a kind of dream to all they said. "Rudolf! Rudolf! Rudolf!" still rang in my ears—a burden of sorrow and of love. At last they saw that I could not heed them, and we walked up and down in silence, till Fritz touched me on the arm, and I saw, a mile or more away, the blue smoke of the train. Then I held out a hand to each of them.

"We are all but half men this morning," said I, smiling. "But we have been men, eh, Sapt and Fritz, old friends? We have run a good course between us."

"We have defeated traitors and set the king firm on his throne," said Sapt.

Then Fritz von Tarlenheim suddenly, before I could discern his purpose or stay him, uncovered his head and bent as he used to do, and kissed my hand; and as I snatched it away he said, trying to laugh: "Heaven doesn't always make the right men kings!"

Old Sapt twisted his mouth as he wrung my hand.

"The devil has his share in most things," said he.

The people at the station looked curiously at the tall man with the muffled face, but we took no notice of their glances. I stood with my two friends and waited till the train came up to us. Then we shook hands again, saying nothing; and both this time—and, indeed, from old Sapt it seemed strange—bared their heads, and so stood still till the train bore me away from their sight. So that it was thought some great man travelled privately for his own pleasure from the little station that morning; whereas, in truth, it was only I, Rudolf Rassendyll, an English gentleman, a cadet of a good house, but a man of no wealth nor position, nor of much rank. They would have been disappointed to know that. Yet had they known all they would have looked more curiously still. For, be I what I might now, I had been for three months a king; which, if not a thing to be proud of, is, at least, an experience to have undergone. Doubtless I should have thought more of it had there not echoed through the air, from the towers of Zenda that we were leaving far away, into my ears and into my heart the cry of a woman's love—"Rudolf! Rudolf! Rudolf!"

Hark! I hear it now!

22

Present, Past—and Future?

The details of my return home can have but little interest. I went straight to the Tyrol and spent a quiet fortnight—mostly on my back, for a severe chill developed itself; and I was also the victim of a nervous reaction, which made me weak as a baby. As soon as I had reached my quarters I sent an apparently careless postcard to my brother, announcing my good health and prospective return. That would serve to satisfy the inquiries as to my whereabouts, which were probably still vexing the prefect of the police of Strelsau. I let my moustache and imperial grow again; and as hair comes quickly on my face, they were respectable, though not luxuriant, by the time that I landed myself in Paris and called on my friend George Featherly. My interview with him was chiefly remarkable for the number of unwilling but necessary falsehoods that I told, and I rallied him unmercifully when he told me that he had made up his mind that I had gone in the track of Mme de Mauban to Strelsau. The lady, it appeared, was back in Paris but was living in great seclusion—a fact for which gossip found no difficulty in accounting. Did not all the world know of the treachery and death of Duke Michael? Nevertheless George bade Bertram Bertrand to be of good cheer, "for," said he flippantly, "a live poet is better than a dead duke." Then he turned on me and asked: "What have you been doing to your moustache?"

"To tell the truth," I answered, assuming a sly air, "a man now and then has reasons for wishing to alter his appearance. But it's coming on very well again."

"What? Then I wasn't so far out! If not the fair Antoinette, there was a charmer."

"There is always a charmer," said I sententiously.

But George would not be satisfied till he had wormed out of me (he took much pride in his ingenuity) an absolutely imaginary love affair, attended with the proper soupçon of scandal, which had kept me all this time in the peaceful regions of the Tyrol. In return for this narrative, George regaled me with a great deal of what he called "inside information" (known only to diplomatists) as to the true course of events in Ruritania, the plots and counter-plots. In his opinion, he told me with a significant nod, there was more to be said for Black Michael than the public supposed; and he hinted at a well-founded suspicion that the mysterious prisoner of Zenda, concerning whom a good many paragraphs had appeared, was not a man at all, but (here I had some ado not to smile) a woman disguised as a man; and that strife between the king and his brother for this imaginary lady's favour was at the bottom of their quarrel.

"Perhaps it was Mme de Mauban herself," I suggested.

"No!" said George decisively. "Antoinette de Mauban was jealous of her and betrayed the duke to the king for that reason. And, to confirm what I say, it's well known that the Princess Flavia is now extremely cold to the king, after having been most affectionate."

At this point I changed the subject and escaped from George's "inspired" delusions. But if diplomatists never know anything more than they had succeeded in finding out in this instance, they appear to me to be somewhat expensive luxuries.

While in Paris I wrote to Antoinette, though I did not venture to call upon her. I received in return a very affecting letter, in which she assured me that the king's generosity and kindness, no less than her regard for me, bound her conscience to absolute secrecy. She expressed the intention of settling in the country and with-drawing herself entirely from society. Whether she carried out her designs I have never heard; but as I have not met her, or heard news of her up to this time, it is probable that she did. There is no doubt that she was deeply attached to the Duke of Strelsau; and her conduct at the time of his death proved that no knowledge of the man's real character was enough to root her regard for him out of her heart.

I had one more battle left to fight—a battle that would, I knew, be severe and was bound to end in my complete defeat. Was I not back from the Tyrol without having made any study of its inhabitants, institutions, scenery, fauna, flora, or other features? Had I not simply wasted my time in my usual frivolous, good-for-nothing way? That was the aspect of the matter which, I was obliged to admit, would present itself to my sister-in-law; and against a verdict based on such evidence I had really no defence to offer. It may be supposed, then, that I presented myself in Park Lane in a shamefaced, sheepish fashion. On the whole my reception was not so alarming as I had feared. It turned out that I had done, not what Rose wished, but—the next best thing—what she prophesied. She had declared that I should make no notes, record no observations, gather no materials. My brother, on the other hand, had been weak enough to maintain that a really serious resolve had at length animated me.

When I returned empty-handed, Rose was so occupied in triumphing over Burlesdon that she let me down quite easily, devoting the greater part of her reproaches to my failure to advise my friends of my whereabouts.

"We've wasted a lot of time trying to find you," she said.

"I know you have," said I. "Half our ambassadors have led weary lives on my account. George Featherly told me so. But why should you have been anxious? I can take care of myself."

"Oh, it wasn't that," she cried scornfully, "but I wanted to tell you about Sir Jacob Borrodaile. You know he's got an embassy— at least, he will have in a month—and he wrote to say he hoped you would go with him."

"Where's he going to?"

"He's going to succeed Lord Topham at Strelsau," said she. "You couldn't have a nicer place, short of Paris."

"Strelsau! H'm!" said I, glancing at my brother.

"Oh, that doesn't matter!" exclaimed Rose impatiently. "Now, you will go, won't you?"

"I don't know that I care about it!"

"Oh, you're too exasperating!"

"And I don't think I can go to Strelsau. My dear Rose, would it be—suitable?"

"Oh, nobody remembers that horrid old story now."

Upon this I took out of my pocket a portrait of the King of Ruritania. It had been taken a month or two before he ascended the throne, and he wore a full beard. Nevertheless she could not miss my point when I said, putting it into her hands: "In case you've not seen or not noticed a picture of Rudolf V, there he is. Don't you think they might recall the story if I appeared at the court of Ruritania?"

My sister-in-law looked at the portrait, and then at me.

"Good gracious!" she said and flung the photograph down on the table.

"What do you say, Bob?" I asked.

Burlesdon got up, went to a corner of the room, and searched in a heap of newspapers. Presently he came back with a copy of the *Illustrated London News*. Opening the paper, he displayed a double-page engraving of the Coronation of Rudolf V at Strelsau. The photograph and the picture he laid side by side. I sat at the table fronting them, and as I looked I grew absorbed. My eye travelled from my own portrait to Sapt, to Strakencz, to the rich robes of the cardinal, to Black Michael's face, to the stately figure of the princess by his side. Long I looked and eagerly. I was roused by my brother's hand on my shoulder. He was gazing down at me with a puzzled expression.

"It's a remarkable likeness, you see," said I. "I really think I had better not go to Ruritania."

Rose, though half convinced, would not abandon her position.

"It's just an excuse," she said pettishly. "You don't want to do anything. Why, you might become an ambassador!"

"I don't think I want to be an ambassador," said I.

"It's more than you ever will be," she retorted.

That is very likely true, but it is not more than I have been. The idea of being an ambassador could scarcely dazzle me. I had been a king!

So pretty Rose left us in dudgeon, and Burlesdon, lighting a cigarette, looked at me still with that curious gaze.

"That picture in the paper—" he said.

"Well, what of it? It shows that the king of Ruritania and your humble servant are as like as two peas."

My brother shook his head.

"I suppose so," he said. "But I should know you from the man in the photograph."

"And not from the picture in the paper?"

"I should know the photograph from the picture. The picture's very like the photograph, but—"

"Well?"

"It's more like you," said my brother.

My brother is a good man and true—so that, for all that he is a married man and mighty fond of his wife, he should know any secret of mine. But this secret was not mine, and I could not tell it to him.

"I don't think it's so much like me as the photograph," said I boldly. "But anyhow, Bob, I won't go to Strelsau."

"No, don't go to Strelsau, Rudolf," said he.

And whether he suspects anything, or has a glimmer of the truth, I do not know. If he has he keeps it to himself, and he and I never refer to it.

And we let Sir Jacob Borrodaile find another attaché.

Since all these events whose history I have set down happened, I have lived a very quiet life at a small house which I have taken in the country. The ordinary ambitions and aims of men in my position seem to me dull and unattractive. I have little fancy for the whirl of society, and none for the jostle of politics. Lady Burlesdon utterly despairs of me. My neighbours think me an indolent, dreamy, unsociable fellow. Yet I am a young man, and sometimes I have a fancy—the superstitious would call it a presentiment—that my part in life is not yet altogether played; that, somehow and some day, I shall mix again in great affairs, I shall again spin policies in a busy brain, match my wits against my enemies', brace my muscle to fight a good fight and strike stout blows. Such is the tissue of my thoughts as, with gun or rod in hand, I wander through the woods or by the side of the stream. Whether the fancy will be fulfilled I cannot tell—still less whether the scene that, led by memory, I lay for my new exploits will be the true one—for I love to see myself once again in the crowded streets of Strelsau, or beneath the frowning keep of the castle of Zenda.

Thus led, my broodings leave the future and turn back on the past. Shapes rise before me in long array—the wild first revel with the king, the rush with my brave tea table, the night in the moat, the pursuit in the forest; my friends and my foes, the people who learned to love and honour me, the desperate men who tried to kill me. And from amid these last comes one who alone of all of them yet moves on earth, though where I know not, yet plans (as I do not doubt) wickedness, yet turns women's hearts to softness and men's to fear and hate. Where is young Rupert of Hentzau—the boy who came so nigh to beating me? When his name comes into my head I feel my hand grip and the blood move quicker through my veins; and the hint of Fate—the presentiment—seems to grow stronger and more definite, and to whisper insistently in my ear that I have yet a hand to play with young Rupert; therefore I exercise myself in arms and seek to put off the day when the vigour of youth must leave me.

One break comes every year in my quiet life. Then I go to Dresden, and there I am met by my dear friend and companion Fritz von Tarlenheim. Last time his pretty wife Helga came, and a lusty crowing baby with her. And for a week Fritz and I ate together, and I hear all of what falls out in Strelsau; and in the evenings, as we walk and smoke together, we talk of Sapt, and of the king, and often of young Rupert; and, as the hours grow small, at last we speak of Flavia. For every year Fritz carries with him to Dresden a little box; in it lies a red rose, and round the stalk of the rose is a slip of paper with the words written: "Rudolf—Flavia—always." And the like I send back by him. That message, and the wearing of the rings, are all that now bind me and the Queen of Ruritania. For—nobler, as I told her, for the act—she had followed where her duty to her country and her House led her, and is the wife of the king, uniting his subjects to him by the love they bear to her, giving peace and quiet days to thousands by her self-sacrifice. There are moments when I dare not think of it, but there are others when I rise in spirit to where she ever dwells; then I can thank God that I love the noblest lady in the world, the most gracious and beautiful, and that there was nothing in my love that made her fall short in her high duty.

Shall I see her face again—the pale face and the glorious hair? Of that I know nothing. Fate has no hint, my heart no presentiment. I do not know. In this world perhaps—nay, it is likely—never. And can it be that somewhere, in a manner whereof our flesh-bound minds have no apprehension, she and I will be together again, with nothing to come between us, nothing to forbid our love? That I know not, nor wiser heads than mine. But if it be never—if I can never hold sweet converse again with her, or look upon her face, or know from her her love, why, then, this side the grave, I will live as becomes the man whom she loves; and for the other side I must pray a dreamless sleep.